REDEFINED LOVE

A WOMAN DISCOVERED A NEW WORLD WHEN SHE LOST HER WORLD.

This is a work of fiction. Names, character, places and incidents are either the product of the author's imagination or are used fictitiously, and any resemblance to actual persons, living or dead, business establishments, events or locales is entirely coincidental.

CHAPTER 1

Peyton Garret, a 30-year-old Manhattan schoolteacher whose husband Fred Snow had passed away when the couple was on their honeymoon in Thailand, tells her experience.

Peyton never revealed to anyone that Fred had been discovered dead in an abandoned cabin from a heart attack brought on by a combination of Viagra, crack cocaine, and crack.

He vanished two days after their honeymoon in Bangkok began, ending their marriage prematurely. She let him take the lead after breakfast on the second day, but he seemed distant and mentioned lady boys and wanting one in bed with them. He also spoke of things she had never even imagined using like "butt-plugs," "hand-cuffs," and "nipple-clamps," so of course they argued. On the first night he had been unable to "perform," and she had blamed it on the alcohol they had consumed on the plane. They were in a temple complex that day while taking a city tour, and after a while Peyton realized Fred had vanished. After their disagreement about sex, she believed he had taken the wrong route on purpose and was now sitting in a bar drinking. She returned to the hotel after the tour and sat by the pool, waiting for him to show up for dinner. He didn't because she was too angry to take action. Nevertheless, when he hadn't returned by the next morning, she decided to call the police. They suspected he had gone in search

of sex, especially after she told them about their quarrel the day before.

The officer in charge of the investigation was a stunning woman named Mary. Peyton would later learn that Mary was actually 32 years old, despite the fact that she didn't appear a day over 20. Peyton was questioned by Mary, who recorded everything. After they returned to the hotel, they dug through Fred's personal items and found his iPad. They talked about her relationship with Fred and how well-versed she was in his personality. She gradually realized how little she actually knew about him. Peyton was from a very traditional family who believed that having sex between married partners was a serious affair and a very personal one. For this reason, she had never even entertained the idea before being married! Also, it clarified her horror when Fred ever discussed blow-jobs. While Fred appeared to be completely sexually liberated, Mary was able to identify some of his personal items with ease, saying, "Oh, I see he has a goodies bag where he keeps a cock-ring, nipple-clamps, Princess Plug, Tiger Balm, hand-cuffs, short leather paddle, butt-plug plus a few other things." Peyton did not recognize some of the items Fred carried. They also discovered hardcore sex movies, such as bondage and BDSM content, on his iPad. According to Mary, it was typical for men with these tendencies to desire to spend their honeymoon in Thailand so they could engage in these acts by hiring natives. All at once, Peyton felt overpowered, horrified, and depressed.

Her marriage to Fred was the result of a quick courtship. She had just ended a five-year relationship with a fellow university student who was a doctor with a stellar resume and a prosperous New York practice. Their break-up had been painful, and her friends had taken her on a weeklong vacation to Ibiza, where she met Fred. Fred seemed exciting, interesting, funny, and happy-go-lucky, everything she had been looking for in a man. He informed her he worked in the film industry, so when she returned to New York she called him at his studios after waiting three days. After meeting, they fell in love and after three months, when he proposed marriage, she agreed without hesitation! He had never allowed her to enter his studios or apartment, not even once!

She knew nothing about Fred other what he had wanted to tell her, and now that she was in Thailand in the cold light of day, reality appeared to rear its ugly head. He had always picked her up from her house or met her in restaurants. Mary pledged to learn more because it might aid in locating him. Mary said she was delighted for Peyton to stick with her because the two ladies had already developed a certain bond. Peyton did not want to just sit and wait and did not want to be alone in the hotel. They returned to the station in the blue police-issue Honda, where they sat in Mary's office while he worked on the computer, scanning databases and Interpol files all around the world. Peyton used the phone to make a few calls back to New York. It was discovered that Fred's studio was heavily geared toward making porn and that not all of his models were of legal drinking age. He also had a history of

engaging in intense sex and drug sessions that frequently resulted in incarceration, traveling to nations in the far east in pursuit of underage prostitutes. In actuality, he was from Romania and went by the name Fred Snow rather than Fred Snow. a real shock. Peyton also discovered that because his personal assets were well-protected and kept completely separate from his business ventures, she was now extremely wealthy. She was going to inherit well over $25 million in US currency, along with a number of properties all over the world, it was discovered after speaking with her attorney.

At the end of the day, they were no closer to discovering where Fred might have ended up, so they drove back to Mary's house, a little bungalow outside of Bangkok, after a fast lunch of noodles. Mary invited Peyton to stay in her bedroom while she sat on the couch. Peyton undid her jeans and sat up in bed wearing just her pajamas and a T-shirt. She put on her headphones and decided to view a few of Fred's iPad's videos in an effort to better understand him. One hour later, Peyton was sitting in a puddle with her underpants fully soaked through. Before to seeing the three quick movies, she had no idea that such things actually happened. The more she watched, the hotter she got since her nipples were as hard as rocks. She had grown up believing that sex should only be performed between a man and his wife, preferably in a dark bedroom, with the express purpose of having children. Also, she had been taught that it was bad and sinful for women to enjoy sex! She had no idea there was a side to her that these movies were

revealing! She drooled and creamed her pants even more at the sight of two ladies making out, one chained to the bed while the other beat her nipples and pussy with a whip before eating her out.

CHAPTER 2

She had always been taught that that part of her body was totally private and just for using the restroom, so the sight of a girl who was barely 20 years old being restrained while a man with a huge hard on peeled into her rear shocked her. caused her to groan and, for the first time in her life, touch her nipples. Peyton was starting to understand that sex was far more than she had ever imagined. She continued to watch the movie, which had a man spread-eagled on the bed with a chain clamped to his nipples, while a young Asian girl, who looked somewhat like Mary when she was younger, alternated between licking the man's cock and yanking on the chain. The man moaned, but a gag that appeared to be on him prevented him from crying out. Peyton watched as the girl removed the gag, which was in the form of a short, fat cock, sat on the man's face, wriggled on his face, and encouraged him to eat her out. He must have been doing so because the girl moaned and groaned while also roughhousing the man's cock. Peyton feverishly fingered her very wet pussy since she found this to be really sexy. She jerked up when she heard a noise and yanked her hand away. Mary smiled as she stood in the doorway and observed her. That is a very old movie, I was working undercover in your husband's business attempting to get evidence to get him put away, I never got enough, but what I did get was plenty of good

sex and lots of money, she said. I could have been wealthy if I had stayed in the company because I was paid well and my checks never failed to arrive 30 days after a film was recorded. Instead, my supervisors forced me to leave. Pity.'

As Mary approached her seductively while taking off her blouse and letting it fall, Peyton sat there gaping. Her lovely, tiny breasts didn't require any support, and they had black, prominent nipples. She was only wearing her scanty underwear as she sat on the edge of the bed. She grinned at Peyton and moved in to give her a little lip kiss. Peyton melted and returned the kiss with a hunger that she had never felt before. Suddenly, the two women were completely enamored with one another. Peyton's T-shirt was roughly torn off as the iPad was moved out of the way. Peyton was pushed into the bed by Mary, who then smothered her with kisses on her face, lips, eyes, and ears. She stooped down and gently kissed Peyton's nipples; she had never allowed a man, much less a woman, to do that to her. Mary alternately kissed, sucked, and softly bit both nipples while simultaneously roughhousing them. Peyton groaningly found herself hesitantly stroking Mary's breasts as well. Peyton screamed and grasped Mary's breasts more firmly, twisting her nipples in reaction. The Asian woman continued biting and sucking Peyton's nips as her hand moved down to her drenched panties. She then grabbed Peyton's pussy over the panties and stroked it violently.

Unusually for this day and age, Peyton was still virgin at the age of 30. Her extremely conservative and overly enthusiastic

religious upbringing had virtually ensured it, and she had spent the majority of her time in college studying with other students who shared her views in prayer groups. Although the Doctor also hailed from an extremely pious family that valued virginity at the altar, their relationship had been completely celibate. She had no idea what passions, when properly awakened, could be unleashed, but Mary was quickly enlightening her to her potential.

Mary sucked and nibbled Peyton's nipples as her hands toyed with her pussy and buttocks as the two women were tangled up on the bed with their underwear on the floor. Peyton was overcome by the feelings and pleasures she was experiencing, so she returned the favor by awkwardly stroking and nibbling Mary's nipples. However, Peyton was picking up quickly, and she was directed in her touches by Mary's hands and groans. Mary slowly and methodically flicked her clitoris, leaving Peyton completely saturated.

Peyton squealed as the feeling was like electricity to her. This simply encouraged Mary to do the motion again and to continue flicking steadily, as if on a drum. Peyton trembled and gasped; she found this to be almost intolerable! Mary could feel that her pussy was ready and yearning for more, so with grim determination, she inserted two fingers inside Peyton's smooth pussy. Mary felt resistance a few centimeters inside the pussy; she had never stolen anyone's virginity before and was unaware that this was Peyton's hymen. As Peyton screamed and her fingers buried themselves into the knuckles, something suddenly gave way as Mary

withdrew and then pushed again, harder this time. As Peyton's moans evolved into cries of pleasure and abandonment, her fingers slid in and out of the engorged pussy. Mary felt the hole widen for her when a third finger joined the first two.

She had never encountered this before, but she was eager to learn. Peyton was lost to her delight. In spite of all she had ever been taught, she gently penetrated the Asian girl's pussy with her own hand. God, it felt good! She poked her fingers into the Asian pussy while she dug into Mary's clitoris, which she had previously discovered during her exploration. The bed was covered in pussy juice, and the two women were wailing and wailing.

Peyton suddenly and unexpectedly felt heat radiating from her innermost essence through her body. The build-up was unavoidable and seemed to begin at her clit, making her toes curl. Mary realized this and quickened the pace, clit-flicking and pussy-pumping in and out. Peyton flung her head back and let out a groan that appeared to originate from the pit of her stomach since she was unable to continue fingering Mary on her own. As the pleasure increased, her body began to shake, she began to perspire profusely, and her nipples began to throb and pulse like two boulders. Her first orgasm in 30 years suddenly struck her, like an express train bursting out of a tunnel! She had the impression that she was falling out of a plane at 10,000 feet in free fall. Mary softly lowered her back to the ground while carefully and slowly pulling back her fingers. Mary rubbed her face, eyes, ears, breasts, and of

course pussy with kisses. After that, she rocked Peyton to sleep while holding her close. Finally reaching adulthood, Peyton.

CHAPTER 3

When morning arrived, Mary was still snuggled up with Peyton when she awoke. She gave Mary a gentle face kiss because she owed this girl an orgasm after the spectacular incident the previous evening. Peyton kissed Mary's naked stomach and nipples as she stirred, working her way down to the pussy. Mary opened her eyes, grinned, and then relaxed while waiting for the New Yorker to do the same for her. Peyton tried to flick Mary's clit with her tongue while kissing her butt. At first, she was a little awkward, but practice makes perfect, and determination makes it happen even faster. Mary required little effort to reach a high state of arousal because she had already been sufficiently primed the previous evening. Peyton pierced the Asian woman's pussy with two fingers while playing with her clit with her tongue. She was quite wet, making it easy for her fingers to move in and out. It didn't take Mary long to begin to tremble and shudder as her imminent climax drew nearer. Peyton now alternated between licking and biting the clit and tongue-fucking the pussy. Mary began making unusual noises when she heard an odd noise, and as a result, she began shaking violently and lifted her arse off the bed, which only made Peyton more desperate to make her cum. She reached up and grasped Mary's breasts while also biting and chewing at her genitalia. This pushed Mary over the edge, and she

screamed and rose off the bed before falling backwards and gasping for air.

Thank you for last night, Peyton said. I tell you the joy was mine; I never dreamed I would ever take another woman's virginity; it truly was a gift, Mary said with a smile.

The two women rested in each other's arms for what felt like an eternity, but they had a long day ahead of them. They got out of bed and returned to the station after breakfast. Nothing seemed to be working despite additional phone calls and computer searches when, in the late afternoon, a male coworker knocked on the door and entered the office. He spoke to Mary in Thai, but it was clear from his glances in Peyton's direction that he was discussing the missing husband. Mary quickly dispatched him from the office after speaking. In a low voice, she said, "It seems this morning there was a raid on several drug addict hangouts and during a chase they ran into an abandoned hut, there they found the death of a Westerner, no ID on him but... " She turned to face Peyton and continued. The idea was clear from Peyton's despondent expression, but Mary wasted no time in acting. She grabbed her wrist as they sprinted to the car and sped off in the direction of the address the male officer had given her. Driving through the seedier areas of the city, where lean-tos and shacks made up the majority of the housing stock, took almost an hour. They eventually spotted a marked police car parked close to a shack where additional officers were moving in and out. Peyton and Mary exited the vehicle and proceeded to the shack. There, she spoke with the

officer manning the door, and they entered. They were overcome by the stench of death when they came upon a white man's decomposing body on the floor, his face contorted into a grimace of misery, naked save for a pair of women's thong underwear, and his now flaccid cock protruding from a cock ring tightly wrapped around his testicles. This was Fred; there was no mistake. Peyton screamed and fled the room, the smell of death catching in her throat. She stood outside and sobbed hysterically as she emptied the contents of her stomach.

"That happens, Peyton; it's not unusual." Peyton wailed while Mary stood next to her and tenderly hugged her. Then, a tissue arrived, and Peyton cleaned her lips. The two women exchanged glances.

What happens next, questioned Peyton? The coroner has already been here and will conduct a Post on the body tonight. I will be told of the results, Mary said. In my country, you would typically be the first suspect and anticipate being detained until an investigation. However, I have spoken on your behalf, and as long as you continue with me, you will be free. Since I've taken on this duty for you, I don't want you to fail me. Peyton spoke gently while crying as she peered into Mary's eyes.

Mary, I swear to you that I had nothing to do with this; in regards to your Peyton in me, you can be confident that I won't betray you. Please ascertain the truth for me. Peyton went right to bed after the women returned to the car and drove gently to Mary's bungalow, where Mary allowed her to sleep.

Mary waited patiently in her living room for the call from her coworkers at the coroner's lab. Until about midnight, she passed the time by watching Thai sitcoms, and she was just about to go to bed when the call arrived.

Fred died of a heart attack, and testing on his blood revealed that he had a cocktail of Viagra, crack, and cocaine in high enough doses to be lethal on their own, let alone when combined. Her contacts also informed her that, during the PM, the police had been looking into reports that Fred had visited a local whorehouse frequented by drug addicts and other undesirables. When the whorehouse was raided, the police discovered additional evidence that Fred had frequented the location for at least the previous ten years. This was neither an accident nor the outcome of a single occurrence. Mary now had the unpleasant duty of telling her new friend—or should we say, "lover"?—the news.

When Peyton woke up alone, she looked at her watch and saw that it was 3 a.m. She wondered where Mary was and if she had heard any news. She also thought about the previous night and started to cry. However, she soon realized that she needed to move on with her life because she had a dead husband to bury and a mystery to solve. Now that she was aware of what she had been missing, she also had a lot of sex to make up for!

She got out of bed and entered the living room wearing only her underwear and a T-shirt. Mary was nowhere to be found. Peyton entered the modest bungalow, which had a kitchen, a bathroom, a living area, and one bedroom. Since there was nowhere to go

within the house, Mary had to leave. The mystery grew when Peyton discovered that the entrance door was locked from the inside. She was positive she could hear groans, shouts, and cracking that sounded like racehorses being beaten. Where could the sounds be coming from if they were so faint and appeared to be in the distance? Peyton was lost in thought as she sat on the couch. As she stood to turn on the TV, she became aware of something that had previously eluded her: a tapestry hanging on the wall next to the TV. She swears the sounds were coming from the tapestry, so she got up, pulled it aside, and discovered it concealed a door. She put her ear to the door, and unmistakably she heard groans, moans, and other noises coming from behind the door.

By turning the handle, Peyton caused the door to silently open outward and lead to a cellar stairway. The sounds of a guy writhing in pain, a whip cracking, and other noises were suddenly fairly loud. The man was being yelled at by Mary. She went down gradually, and when she reached the bottom and could only hear the man, she feared she had gone down into hell. A medieval prison appeared in front of her, complete with whips and chains hanging from the ceiling, rings and bars fastened to the walls, and a metal frame bed in the middle of which a man was lying tied spread-eagled with clamps on his nipples and his cock. The man had obvious signs of recent whipping, including very fresh welts on his belly and thighs. Peyton immediately recognized the scene

as the one from the film she had watched, where she had seen a very young Mary, who was not present.

CHAPTER 4

Mary entered through a doorway in the corner. She looked stunning in a tight leather catsuit that zipped open halfway down her chest, 6 inch stiletto heel ankle boots, her hair tightly tied back, and long leather gloves. "Peyton, my friend, I wanted to talk about this before but I didn't get a chance, events overtook us." 'You see Peyton, I realized how much I loved the lifestyle after I was pulled out of my undercover job in Fred's company and never fully left it. The video you saw with me in it was filmed here in this dungeon; this bungalow was originally the firm's but I got it as part payment for my silence in the police case. I was astonished when Fred showed up in Bangkok because he had too many enemies there and you had just reported him missing. I made it a point to get involved in the investigation, but little did I realize that I would fall madly in love with you since you are a sex-bomb and a hidden world of delights. I have so much to teach you, and you have so much to learn! '

Was it shock as Peyton regarded Mary with fresh eyes? Horror? Disgust? Peyton wanted to be the one restrained and lashed; she wanted to feel the ropes around her wrists and ankles, and she wanted to be surrounded by more than three fingers. Peyton now asked herself, "Where did that yearning come from?" She had seen all of these in Fred's videos on his iPad. She yearned to fulfill all

of his portrayed desires. She had to watch and learn more before realizing that Mary was also a fantastic teacher.

"Mary, I'd be honored if you taught me how to submit, how to take cock in my every hole, how to be a slut, and how to enjoy sex in any manner possible. I want to be used and abused by men like I've seen in Fred's videos, so please tie me up, chain me up, whip me, fuck me, and more! Be my teacher, please.

Peyton saw Mary approaching and took her by the hand. Mary led Peyton over to the man who was lying on the bed and stood her beside him. She then bowed Peyton forward at the waist and directed her mouth toward the man's stiff cock, forcing her mouth around it.

Imagine that you are eating an ice cream, Peyton, and lick his cock-head while bobbling your head and swirling your tongue into its tiny eye. No matter what I do to you, don't stop doing this! If you give up, you will regret it.

Peyton closed her eyes and began to perform the directions. At first, she felt a little queasy, but she overcame it by sucking, licking, poking, and bobbling. Suddenly, she heard a loud "Crack! She heard Mary yell as the pain struck her approximately three seconds later, causing her arse to explode in agony. She stopped sucking and turned to gaze back when she felt another stroke hit her again.

Don't even consider stopping, slut! I advised you to brush him off since stopping will make you regret it. If you don't want to regret it, keep going! Peyton continued sucking while Mary continued to

beat her in the arse. As tears streamed down her face, the man's cock began to tremble. Peyton had never given a blow-job, so she had no idea what this meant, so she continued. Suddenly, her mouth began to fill with thick, acrid semen. Mary was holding her face firmly over the cock, and all she could hear was him telling her to swallow "every single drop!" which she dutifully carried out.

Mary talked in the same soothing tones as the previous night as she straightened her up, turned her around, and gave her the most passionate kisses.

Peyton, my lovely little butterfly, you've done a great job. You'll make a great student, and it will be a pleasure to teach you. But now, a little reward.

The two women made their way to the end of the dungeon and through the dim doorway in the corner. One was short, Asian, and very attractive. The other was tall, Western, and equally attractive. This was Mary's personal retreat; it included a magnificent four-poster bed, a closet filled with exotic clothing, soft leather floggers, and silk ropes strewn throughout the space. Mary brought Peyton to the bed and stripped her before placing her on it. After giving Peyton a gentle kiss on the neck and face, Peyton relaxed and grinned. Mary softly bit and sucked on Peyton's nipples while pausing long enough to raise Peyton's arms above her head. Mary fastened her hands to the headboard, which was covered with a variety of secret rings, ropes, and straps. Peyton surprisedly kicked out, but Mary immediately bound her legs with

a few covert straps. Peyton was now where she wanted her to be. Peyton put the cuffs to the test and discovered that she was firmly confined to the bed. Peyton yelled in shock and anguish as Mary bit harder on her nipples, yanking them away from her body. Mary paused and pulled something from the nightstand before speaking. It pains my little butterfly, don't it? You want Mary, your friend, to stop? Unfortunately, Mistress B, who won't stop, has taken her position and is not currently present. Peyton's eyes widened in terror and disbelief as Mary placed the gag into her mouth and tightened it. As she was saying this, she reached up with a penis gag she had in her hands. Once on Peyton's nipples, Mary took a pair of clamps and turned them just a few times before placing them there. Mary playfully dragged the chain that connected the clamps away from Peyton's body as she wailed and yelled through the gag. Using a remote control, Mary brought down from the ceiling a hook suspended from a chain. She halted it a short distance from the bed and connected it to the chain attached to the nipple clamps, then pushed the hook up a few centimeters to tighten the smaller chain. Peyton struggled to get out of bed to relieve the pressure on her nipples, but Mary had effectively restrained her. Peyton's body remained stiff and arched as Mary grinned and turned his back. Mary had simply gone to retrieve something from a sideboard, something Peyton had never seen at all, when she panicked.

With a small flogger in her hand that had a plaited handle in black and red leather and numerous thin red leather tails, Mary moved

back toward the bed. She came to a stop by the bed and placed the tails on Peyton's chest before slowly dragging them down the body to her trimmed crotch.

Peyton trembled with excitement and need as she felt the thin leather dragging down her hypersensitive body. She was extremely stiff. Mary lowered the tails onto Peyton's pussy and raised the flogger. When she moved it around and gently dangled it, the pussy began to leak juice; it was gleaming and appeared to be honey-glazed. Peyton strained her neck to look down and saw Mary's lovely body playing the flogger on her eager pussy. She had never experienced this before, although she had certainly experienced an aroused and wet pussy in the past. Peyton had also desired sexual pleasure, but her upbringing had always managed to get her to force these thoughts out of her mind. A cold shower would not be able to calm her down, though. But this was extraordinary, and it increased her desire in every pore of her body. She wanted this desperately!

Peyton had never in her life anticipated that she would need another woman's touch as much as she did now. She also had never even vaguely dreamed that one day, while bound to a bed and facing the danger of being whipped, this was Mary's current plan. Nonetheless, Mary continued to play the flogger all over Peyton's body, including her pussy, breasts, and legs. Peyton quavered in longing, unsure of when the next phase would arrive. She had been unable to see the motion of the flogger on her body for a long because she had her eyes closed. She collapsed back

onto the bed once it abruptly stopped and the clamps from her nipples were released. Her eyes suddenly opened.

She had prayed that things wouldn't end there, and she was right. Peyton's muffled cry was simply a foreshadowing of what was to come as Mary gently raised the flogger and brought it down hard on her left breast. In a slow and steady pace, Mary kept repeating the action on the right breast: left, right, left, and so on. Peyton's cries became louder and higher in pitch, but the gag kept them from becoming excessive. In any case, the dungeon was soundproof, so no outside noises could be heard. Just as Mary desired, the nipples engorged and the breasts turned progressively pink. She came to a stop with them and began to flogger Peyton's front till she reached her pussy. There was nothing she could do but endure the flogger as it descended on her own pussy, at first gently but then swiftly harder.

All of a sudden, Mary removed the gag and gave Peyton a passionate kiss. Peyton heaved on the bed. Peyton's wrists and feet were freed of their restraints, and she climbed onto the bed with her. Their hands were entwined, and they were stroking each other's bodies. Mary gradually dropped all her garments as the Asian's bare body was probed by the just discovered sex bomb next to her. While the other girl put her fingers into Peyton's eager and anxious pussy, Peyton experimented with gently kissing and swallowing Mary's nipples. Amazingly moist, it appeared as though Peyton had begun to release the fluids that had built up over her years of fasting and celibacy!

CHAPTER 5

Mary kissed Peyton's entire body, turning gently so that her head was over Peyton's pussy and her own pussy was above Peyton's head. She slowly began to suck and nibble Peyton's private areas as she gently slid herself onto her face. The New Yorker didn't need any directions because the task at hand was clear-cut. While experiencing feelings and sensations that were out of this world, she began kissing and nibbling the Asian's pussy and clit. Peyton reciprocated, and for a good amount of time, Mary's tongue and lips were joined by her fingers exploring Peyton's pussy. Mary noticed that the bed was completely wet and that Peyton was on the verge of losing it. It was time to step it up.

Mary rose from the bed and advised Peyton to remain still. She went to the corner and fiddled with something before turning around to see Mary wearing an exquisite 8 inch strap-on. Mary was now wearing a tight leather harness, which had a large black rubber cock protruding from it with veins and an upward curvature. She was slowly applying lubrication all over it as she moved closer to Peyton. Will she be able to handle that, Peyton breathed in shock? That appeared enormous to her! Mary took Peyton's hand and placed it on the cock as she stood next to the bed. She then curled her fingers around it and stroked it up and down so Peyton could feel its girth and determine its length.

Mary, I'm afraid I've never had anything in my pussy—just your fingertips yesterday, Peyton said quietly. I'm not sure if I can handle something this thick and long.

Peyton, you can and you will!, Mary fiercely commanded. Mary doesn't make the request; Mistress B does! Mary then stepped onto the bed and straddled Peyton, pushing her legs apart and bringing her closer while holding her by the knees. As Mary gently massaged Peyton's labia at the entrance with the big black dildo, pussy honey slowly began to seep out and begin to drip down. Mary inserted the silicone cock into Peyton's gaping mouth slowly, purposefully, and relentlessly. While this continued, Peyton murmured and groused, groaning at each push because she was powerless to stop it from encroaching on her body. Although there wasn't much room, Peyton was drenched.

After some time, Mary managed to get the entire cock inside Peyton's pussy with a lot of groaning, straining, and pain. While Peyton gathered her power as well, she paused to collect her breath. Invisibly, Mary moved the cock out an inch, then pushed it back in again, out an inch and a half, and back in again. Mary gradually increased his speed and intensity as he pulled back and pushed forward. Under her, Peyton squealed in tune with the pushes and made high-pitched screams. Mary forced the cock deeper into Peyton's pussy by pulling back on her knees; she then almost entirely pulled it out before repeatedly ramming it back in. Peyton was very wet, as shown by the squelching sounds.

Mary released her hold on Peyton's knees, squatted down on top of her, and gave her a full mouth kiss while rapidly and violently thrusting the strap-on into Peyton's pussy. Mary's back was scratched by Peyton, who also gave passionate kisses in return.

Mary rotated Peyton's face, bit her earlobe, and dragged it away from her body while biting on her bottom lip and pulling. She wanted Peyton to have something special because she could feel Peyton's pussy trembling beneath her. Mary stopped pumping the cock and stood back up. Peyton pleaded with her to keep going and complete the task she had started, but Mary remained still for a while. With her hands on Peyton's breasts, Mary grinned inwardly as she leaned slightly forward and played with Peyton's nipples by gently tweaking, flicking, and scratching them with her long nails.

Peyton's groans were louder and more intense, and Mary noticed that she was getting very close to breaking. She quickly pounded the enormous black dildo in and out of Peyton's pussy while cruelly twisting her nipples between her thumb and fingertip. Mary released go of the right nipple long enough to slap the American in the face after hearing Peyton scream.

If you scream any louder, I'll choke you and tie you up so tightly that you won't be able to move your toes!

The torture was resumed by Mary, who alternated twisting and yanking the nipple away from Peyton's body. Mary was pushing Peyton toward her inevitable orgasm as the dildo was flying in and out of the pussy.

Both ladies could feel it coming as it surged like an oncoming wave, gaining strength and velocity as it steadily ascended higher and higher. It was neither sudden nor unexpected. Peyton could feel the orgasm beginning in the pit of her stomach, a rumble that

shook her to the core. The warmth slowly traveled down to her intestines before finding its way to her pussy, where it quickly broke over her. Wave after wave of pleasure soon followed, and she was unable to stop yelling and chanting Mary's name.

Mary screamed as she approached, flopped forward over Peyton's body, and gave her a deep kiss while they hugged and exchanged glances. This was to mark the beginning of something positive.

As Peyton awoke, she discovered that she was the only person in the boudoir. She discreetly got up and left the room. The dungeon was deserted, and there was silence everywhere. She returned to the main level through the stairs and entered Mary's usual bedroom, where she was found sleeping alone. When Peyton looked at her watch, she noticed that it was getting close to six thirty in the morning. There was a glimmer of daylight. As Mary's voice interrupted her, she glanced around.

Mary joined Peyton and said, "My little butterfly has awakened from her sleep. Let's prepare some coffee and talk." Mary also gave Peyton a T-shirt to put on. Both girls entered the kitchen and set to work brewing a pot of coffee. With their cups in hand, they sat at the kitchen counter and gradually shared their life experiences up to that point over the next hour or so.

Peyton, who was born Peyton Constance Garret, was raised in a strict, devout Catholic household. Her two older brothers, Jerry Francis and John Fitzgerald, were both lawyers in prominent Manhattan firms, and her younger sister, Rose Elizabeth, had joined a religious order and was currently serving as a missionary

in Peru. Rose Elizabeth lived in Cusco, high in the Andes mountains, not far from Macchu Picchu. The family was undoubtedly a fan of the Samuels! While her mother continued to teach piano at a very prestigious Catholic school operated by nuns, her father was a retired police captain in the NYPD. Peyton herself was raised in the Upper East Side and baptized at the Church of Saint Ignatius of Loyola, a place she frequently visited and proudly recalled as the location of Jacqueline Samuel's funeral.

The nuns were strict, and Peyton had been a boisterous, fun-loving girl who frequently got into trouble despite being academically successful. Peyton had attended the same school that her mother worked at and had been subjected to the strict regime. She was no stranger to the paddle, cane, or leather belt, having endured all three as well as countless over-the-knee hand-spankings during her school years. She started attending the school when she was just five years old and left when she was eighteen to attend Harvard, where she received a top ranking. Her undergraduate years had been filled with a lot of effort and late-night studies. There had been men, for sure, but they had always been good Catholic men who respected her desire to stay chaste and accompanied her to Sunday mass at the Memorial Church. Several boys had stayed far away from her after recognizing her type from her conservative appearance and large attendance.

She had met Jerry, a charming boy, at the conclusion of her stay at Harvard.

CHAPTER 6

They dated a few times but felt the timing was off because she didn't want to hurt his chances in his chosen career and he didn't want to have to share his late nights of hard work as an intern. He came from a wealthy family in Boston and was studying medicine. Before the relationship ever began, they split up. Yet as fate would have it, four years later Peyton attended a coworker's wedding and ran across Jerry once more. He proposed that they go on a date once more while working in his father's incredibly successful practice. Peyton was welcomed with open arms. It was a relationship straight out of a romance novel, with fancy dinners, strolls around the park, and moonlit kisses. That ended there. No rummaging into sweaters, no lover's lane in the car, no rear row in the theater. No sex, regardless of size, shape, or form. And it succeeded. so it appeared.

For five years, fun-loving Peyton and serious, hardworking Jerry engaged in this. Their relationship was certain to fail because they were both too serious and hard workers. The previous six months had been a living hell, with argument after argument. Peyton adored Jerry with all of her heart and soul, but she yearned for a little bit more excitement. She wanted more hot dogs in the park rather than Filet Mignon at the Waldorf-Astoria. Jerry merely want an attractive face and a well-groomed body to flaunt next to him. Peyton's friends kept urging her to break up with Jerry, but she was too obstinate to do so. Then, unexpectedly, it happened. Jerry broke up with her by email, saying that he had fled to Mexico

with his medical nurse, a curvy 20-year-old blonde. Peyton was devastated and hurt, and Jerry's parents naturally blamed her, saying that she hadn't shown their son enough love. Her head teacher scheduled her for a counseling session and given her a month's worth of homework for "anxiety and despair," because she felt like she needed it. She simply went through the motions of living during the days and spent the nights sobbing herself to sleep. After that, her pals came to a consensus. They all made reservations for a week in Ibiza, and then they virtually had to drag Peyton onto the plane. She met Fred there, and the rest is history, as they say. Except for certain information Peyton might provide later.

Mary was enthralled by this tale; she had been holding Peyton's hand the entire time, and tears streamed down her face. Mary hugged Peyton and gave her a loving kiss on the cheek while making hushed noises to her. Peyton clung to Mary closely as she expressed her gratitude for her assistance and enquired about her. Mary, also known as Mary Watt, was found abandoned in a cardboard box with her name and birthdate written on it on the steps of the neighborhood police station in one of the villages in Phuket Province. She was covered in an old blanket at the time. She was discovered by an elderly police officer named Sarawut Yamnam as he was leaving work one morning. Because he and his wife Sudarat had never had children of their own and because the local authorities in this region of Thailand were so weak and lax, he scooped up the infant and took her to his house. The couple

claimed that the child was a niece that they had been put in charge of raising; in this region of the world, obtaining a birth certificate was not difficult. They raised her as one of their own, showing her love, care, and harsh discipline. Mary needed to be controlled because she had a propensity to act erratically. She was caught robbing the market's vegetable stalls at the age of five, but it was quickly overlooked until she repeated the offense five times in one week, robbing not only the fruit but also the change from the money drawers. The stall owner who caught her had taken her home after dragging her there so Sudarat could hear the tale and take Mary in by the ear. Mary was placed over her knees as she sat down on the kitchen chair after dragging her inside. She hand-spanked the little girl on her bottom while pulling up her thin dress. Mary sobbed and cried, but Sudarat persisted until she was content. The elderly woman then gave the young girl a hug and soothed her, telling her softly that decent girls don't steal.

Sadly, Mary had a tendency to steal; she would take anything that caught her eye, including shiny jewelry, booths, and shops. By the time Sudarat was 10, they had switched to the leather belt and strap every time she discovered she had been soundly paddled. This didn't really make a difference because the elderly couple was struggling to cope and it was tough for Sudarat and Sarawut to use the strap efficiently. Mary was transferred to a stringent Catholic school operated by nuns at the conclusion of her ninth summer after Sarawut made a few inquiries through his contacts

in the police. Peyton grinned at this because the females were so different yet similar in other ways.

Mary struggled in school because she was not used to being held to such stringent rules. Instead of being required to study, she would have liked to be running about the streets with other street kids and stealing fruit. She frequently found herself in hot water and the target of a leather strap or rattan cane. She nearly started to miss it when a day went by without at least a stroke of the strap on her hands because her buttocks almost always bore the signs of a harsh beating.

The elder girls were then given a chat by a policewoman when they were sixteen years old. Only Mary maintained utter silence during the discussion. She diligently studied math, Thai, and English throughout the course of the following two years. Since she kept up her antics and cheek, the spankings naturally continued, but her academic performance vastly improved.

At the age of 18, she completed her education and applied to join the Royal Thai Police. She did well on the entrance exams as well as the physical and psychological evaluations. She received preparation for her interview from one of her teachers, and she aced it with ease. The following two months were divided between her helping Sudarat around the house during the day and socializing with friends at night. She was well-behaved and avoided mischief successfully.

Three days before the two-month period came to an end, she received a formal letter. She'd been welcomed in!

CHAPTER 7

The bad news was that she would have to go to police academy in Bangkok before being put in charge of a unit at the conclusion of her training. When their daughter, Mary Watt (this was the name she now preferred), left in uniform to board the airplane to Bangkok, Sarawut and Sudarat were extremely proud of her.

She was assigned to a Bangkok unit after her six months of training, where she promptly rose to the position of top recruit. She worked hard, became a lance-corporal by the time she was twenty, a corporal by the time she was twenty-two, and a sergeant by the time she was twenty-five. Her cunning and understanding of the underworld contributed to her success. She put forth a lot of effort both at work and play, enjoying her nights as Peyton now understood. In the days to come, Mary will provide more information about this.

Mary sobbed as she related to Peyton how Sudarat was in an elderly facility back in Phuket and Sarawut had passed away just a year before. The two females hugged one other while sobbing. In the days to come, they would still have a ton more to share with one another.

The two lovers needed to return to the station because it was getting close to eight o'clock. Mary was too small for any of Peyton's regular clothing to suit her; she only had last night's attire and her luggage were still at the motel. The only items Peyton was able to borrow were a g-string (which was a bit tight and barely covered her pubic area!) and a kaftan, which on Peyton reached to

just below her buttocks; thus, she would have to be careful not to bend down too quickly. She made the decision to forgo last night's dirty bra and hoped her pert breasts would be good. Mary changed into her uniform before they entered the vehicle.

Peyton found the hour-long journey to the station to be incredibly interesting because she was getting to see a side of Bangkok that few visitors ever did. A macho man in the car next to them started to make advances toward Peyton at a set of lights since he saw she was without a bra. Mary frowned at him and used the chance to grab Peyton's breast to demonstrate that it was hers. He gave in. When Peyton moved her hand down her pussy and touched it through the kaftan and panties, she was about to say something to Mary. Peyton flushed because Mary continued to stroke and caress her despite the fact that it was daytime.

When they arrived at the station, Peyton's borrowed g-string was completely soaked through. She was also fairly certain that her kaftan had a wet spot, but she was pulled into the station and taken to her office before she could react. She was positive that everyone was looking behind her. As soon as they were inside, Mary locked the door and shut it. She then turned Peyton to face her and gave her a passionate kiss while biting her bottom lip and pulling it away from her body. The two girls merged into one writhing mass once Peyton reciprocated the kiss. Mary kneaded Peyton's breasts when she was wearing a kaftan. She wanted to play with them physically, but she reasoned that there would be plenty of time afterwards. She said one thing,

Peyton nodded gravely as Mary unlocked the office door, "Tonight we trim and shave this, I want only a very thin landing strip of stubble." The Criminal Investigation section had a witness who had spotted a black van at the shanty where Fred's body had been found, she learned after making a few calls. Using the van's number, they were able to locate a narcotics dealer in Bangkok's central business district. He was now being questioned by police while being held in prison. Mary called Peyton's hotel while this was going on, made arrangements for her luggage to be delivered to the station, checked her lover out, and canceled the room account. Peyton sat in a corner and stared off into space, lost in thought and unsure of what might occur next. Mary answered the ringing phone and barked down the phone while speaking in Thai. As she turned to face Peyton, she thanked the caller and hung up. "Peyton, the man we have in custody has confessed to giving your husband crack after giving him a deadly injection of Viagra and cocaine on purpose. As this guy burst in, Fred was reportedly bound to a rack; he had a personal matter to settle with him and was aware of Fred's presence. Fred kept avoiding him since he owed him money for using underage prostitutes in his movies. The situation was made worse when the guy lit a crack pipe and forced Fred to smoke it after being unsatisfied with Fred's responses. He then injected the drugs as a scare tactic but unintentionally used too much. Peyton listened intently, sad but also relieved that the truth had come out; she had been proven innocent and now wanted to leave and return to New York, but what about Mary? Fred had

a seizure and died there on the rack, so together with the whore he had been with they carried Fred's body out to the black van we traced, drove him downtown, and dumped him in the shack. Peyton had not heard a word that the Asian had been saying.

'Peyton! Do you fully grasp what I just said? You are exonerated of all charges, and Fred's body will be released by the coroner this afternoon. We need to make arrangements; you can either have it shipped or flown back to the United States, or you can choose to bury him here. Alternatively, you can choose to have him cremated and only fly with the ashes. Peyton was hypnotized; she did not want to approach the body of her perverse husband, but she knew she couldn't just leave him here because he had family. She decided right away,

Mary nodded in agreement, "I want Fred cremated as soon as possible; I'll carry the ashes back to the US with me."

'I'll make it happen!

She then called, stating, "The cremation will be in five days, nothing is available sooner," and after a short while hung up.

Mary raced around her desk to hold Peyton tightly and rock her gently as she sobbed uncontrollably after getting up and grinning at her. She bawled endlessly, trying to communicate through the sobs while making incomprehensible noises. Mary embraced her until she finally stopped. Mary sat her down and picked up her phone once more. She spoke quickly into the phone, hung up, and then placed another brief call. Finally, she stood and addressed Peyton.

CHAPTER 8

Peyton's face lightened up as Mary said, "I've taken the week off; I'll stay with you till after the cremation, that is, if you want me to."

"I'm grateful for everything. I adore you so much, my sweetest angel! How could I possibly repay you! She tightly gripped Mary until the other girl pulled her away.

Oh, have no worry, my little butterfly, you will repay me in many ways before you depart Bangkok. With that, Mary took Peyton's hand and led her out of the office and out of the station. As the pair went hand in hand, got into the car, and sped away, all eyes were on them.

Peyton's luggage was waiting for them when they arrived at her home because one of Mary's phone calls had arranged to have it transported there rather than to the police station. Peyton opened them after spending the next hour separating Fred's clothes from hers. Fred's clothes all went into a bin liner to be dumped, while her clothes all went into an empty closet Mary had offered her. Mary remained in the background since she thought Peyton needed some privacy during this time. She passed the time by placing a few covert calls.

Peyton entered the living room and sat next to Mary on the sofa after finishing her work, which was already late in the afternoon. She leaned in for a quick kiss, which Mary returned before moving her hands over Peyton's body and removing the kaftan and T-shirt both of them were wearing. They were both sitting there in their

underwear—Peyton in a borrowed g-string and Mary in a thong. Peyton had a firm pair of 36 inch "C" cups that stood proudly out considering their size, while Mary had breasts more typical of her culture, displaying a perky set of 34 inch "A" cups. Both girls were proud of their breasts. Peyton's nipples, which were about two inches in circumference and as thick as the tip of her little finger, were a deep purple color. On the other hand, Mary's were a delicate pink color, resembling pencil erasers, and her areola was barely an inch in size. It was truly the first time they were allowed to gaze at one other in the light, and they liked what they saw. They paused and exchanged longing glances. Mary lovingly stroked Peyton's breasts, running her fingertips over each golden lobe. She drew her nails around the areola in circles, getting ever-closer to the nipples while never quite striking them or missing them either. Peyton trembled; it was like lightning; she had not seen the nails contact her nipples yet a ripple had raced right through each breast! Peyton's nails almost imperceptibly brushed the base of one nipple, then the other, before floating over the nipples themselves.

Mary persisted in his assault on Peyton's stunning breasts, increasing the frequency, intensity, and persistence of his nipple-scratching. Then the pulling, tweaking, and pinching started. Peyton first groan, then groaned, and last screamed out in both anguish and joy. Inviting Peyton to follow, Mary stood up. Both females undid their underwear before climbing onto the bed as they descended into the dungeon and the boudoir. Peyton wriggled

and cried out as Mary continued to play with her lover's breasts and nipples. Mary halted, then took Peyton's arms and dragged them toward the bed's corners, locking them there with Velcro straps. Peyton couldn't get out of bed until Mary allowed her to.

Peyton heard water running and the sound of metal as Mary left, and then her Asian companion returned bringing a little bowl and other items. Mary said.

As she spoke, she picked up an electric trimmer and set it on 2mm, running it over Peyton's pussy until it was even all over. "My butterfly is now going to lose most of her pussy hair, I want this little hole to be kept trim and almost hairless, as a tribute to me and as a way to ensure we both get the maximum pleasure," she said. She then moistened the entire hairy pussy with warm water with a washcloth, created a lather with an antique shaving brush, and rubbed the lather into each individual hair. Mary worked her way towards the pussy slit slowly and cautiously, taking care not to completely shave Peyton's pussy. She left a thin strip just above the labia, or what Peyton had heard her friends refer to as a "landing strip," when they shaved their bikini lines. After shaving, Mary used the washcloth to remove all suds and hairs before thoroughly rubbing hydrating Aloe Vera gel into the entire area.

She experienced a variety of odd feelings as a result of the workout, and she was convinced she saw liquid trickling out of her hole and that her clit was standing up. She wasn't sure if she wanted Mary to stop and let her cool down or if she wanted her to keep going and get into a frenzy like last night. He felt a kiss on

her pussy and then more and more as she was ready to speak. Mary used her tongue to play with the freshly shaved pussy's labia and clit before untying her and turning her onto her front. She again buckled her back to the bed and continued to eat her out, pausing every now and then to rub her labia, pussy, and asshole with her fingers. Then she abruptly came to a stop. Peyton was able to speak a few words.

'Noooo! Continue on! I need it immediately, so please eat me out and give me joy! When Mary merely stood there and watched, she shook her head dejectedly. She placed a ball-gag into Peyton's lips and buckled it firmly behind her head. Peyton struggled with her restraints, but they were strong. Mary said firmly,

My tiny butterfly, please! All this demanding and yelling! You need direction, control, and discipline because I believe it has been too long since you were under the harsh tutelage of the nuns. in particular, discipline. I'll have to take care of that! Mary then left and entered the main dungeon. Under the gag, Peyton continued to struggle and make noise. In the adjacent room, Mary could be heard moving around and opening cabinets. When she returned a short while later, Peyton was able to turn her head, and her blood immediately froze. Mary was holding a leather paddle in one hand and a two-foot-long tawse with a split at the bottom 10 inches in the other. She approached Peyton after putting the tawse on the sideboard against the wall.

Peyton uttered a low groan as Mary raised the paddle and gently lowered it to land on her left buttock.

CHAPTER 9

On her right buttock, she repeated the action. Long periods of medium swats on alternate buttocks were continued by Mary. Splat... splat... splat... continues forever. As far as the gag would allow, Peyton's grunts grew louder and louder. She raised her head and fiercely shook it, but to no purpose. Swats continued, and the ass became a darker and darker pink tint by the minute. It ceased after what felt like an eternity. Mary placed her palm on the left buttock and felt the heat radiate as she ran her nails over the now-red buttocks. She loudly slapped Peyton's right cheek, and Peyton shrieked despite the gag. The Asian girl believed that things were going well and that it was time to move on.

Mary took up the tawse and set the paddle on the sideboard before speaking.

"Peyton, I'm going to reacquaint you with the sensation of having the tawse used on your ass while you were in school. In fact, you may have forgotten how it feels. About fifteen minutes ago, a leather paddle was lightly rubbed against your behind. While being bound and muzzled, you struggled to cry and shout. I'll now untie you and take off the gag before giving you 20 tawse strokes, 10 on each buttock. If you take them well—without resisting or yelling or otherwise trying to stop me—I'll reward you; if not, you'll regret it.

Peyton hastily nodded as tears started to form in her eyes. She longed for this to be over and for Mary to be holding her and loving her. else did she? Peyton realized she didn't want it to end

as she gave it more thought and waited longer for Mary to continue. She felt her nipples throb, her skin tingle, and her pussy get extremely wet; she craved to feel the tawse; she felt more alive than ever. Old recollections had been sparked by the paddle.

Twelve-year-old Peyton sneaked out of her room at Saint Brigid's and crept down the hallways to meet her friend Annie. They were going to share some chocolates Annie's mother had given her. She pondered why she hadn't yet met up with her as she descended the stairs to Annie's floor; the girl must have miscalculated the time! It was completely dark when Peyton went down to Annie's dorm and quietly opened the door. Peyton snuck over to Annie's bed, where the foolish girl was sound asleep. When the dorm lights suddenly went on, Peyton was going to slap her awake as she approached her aggressively. Peyton noticed that Annie was not in bed—a bunched-up pillow was there instead. Sister Mary Agnes and Sister Mary Kildare were standing there when she heard a severe voice calling her name. Poor Annie was standing between them, her face covered in fear. The other female students in the dorm were all sitting up in bed, keeping their mouths tightly closed.

After being led in a march to the Sisters' study, Annie and she were ordered to take off their nightgowns and pajamas and lean against the desk. The girls' asses were smacked with leather paddles that the Sisters had taken turns using. They yelled and shouted in pain, tears streaming down their cheeks, but the nuns continued to beat the girls despite the fact that their butts burned and felt like they

shoulder. then swiftly lowered it to Peyton's left buttock. Mary continued to strike Peyton with the tawse on alternate buttocks as Peyton clenched her teeth and gripped the cushion hard. Even though Peyton's eyes were squeezed up, tears were still streaming down her cheeks. She was so focused on acting properly that she was not even aware the beating had ended. Peyton's ass throbbed in agony, felt enormous, and she was unable to even comprehend what it looked like.

Mary kissed her softly everywhere her tawse had gone, making Peyton feel loved. She felt butterfly kisses all over her ass. Her lips were replaced by fingers covered in calming Aloe gel, which was applied to her buttocks, crack, and rubbed slowly into her tormented skin. The Asian's fingers infiltrated Peyton's openings covertly, at first subtly but then becoming increasingly invasive. Peyton's clit was not forgotten either; those dexterous fingers paid it a visit and flicked the engorged bundle of nerve endings. Peyton groaningly yelped and shrieked occasionally in delight and surprise. She was constantly gushing juice and was certain that if the intensity increased, she would orgasm.

Peyton pondered what was going to happen as the fingers spread a chilly, slick liquid within her asshole—presumably lubrication. Mary's finger rubbed the lube well into and around Peyton's asshole. After briefly occupying herself with the nightstand drawer, Mary held a small object in front of Peyton's eyes so she could see it.

CHAPTER 10

When Mary informed her that it was a Princess Plug, she stopped wondering about the object because it resembled a silver teardrop with a jeweled base. Peyton had never seen one and was unsure of its function.

When it touched her asshole coldly, she immediately realized where it was going to go. As the Princess was being pushed in slowly, she was ready to object when she thought of Mary's warning; instead, she remained silent and bit her teeth. She made an effort to untense her muscles, but she was up against her mind, which was fighting the invasion. Peyton exhaled through clenched teeth as Mary relaxed and took the PP out an inch. Then Mary pressed in again, this time going a little bit deeper before pulling it out once more. The sphincter was now twitching and gaping a half inch as she paused, with the PP resting on it. After one more, resolute push, the PP was able to slide past her sphincter and into her. Peyton had never had anything in her ass because, throughout her childhood, it had only been used for pooping. In fact, she had never even seen her own asshole in its entirety, let alone with a lump of steel inside. She was enjoying it, too!

Peyton squirmed and purred like a kitten, and her broad grin suggested that things were looking up.

The two bodies that were entangled on the enormous bed were bathed in sunlight that came through the bedroom window. Both of them had contented expressions. As Mary gradually awoke and

stretched out, she kissed Peyton gently on the face till the American awoke and smiled.

"Mary, you made me a very happy woman last night. You unlocked in me emotions that had been dormant for years, emotions I had first felt as a young adolescent but never returned. Thank you, my friend, my lover, and my Mistress; you broke down barriers I had set up to fit in.' Mary grinned at her new partner and gave her another gentle kiss.

She leaned in for a kiss and said, "Peyton, you are my little butterfly; I have so much to teach you, and it will be my pleasure to do it. And today we learn something new." She then got up, put on a camisole, and spent some time on the phone as Peyton made breakfast. When everything was done, the two laughed and chatted while eating at the bar. As the females were done, Mary spoke to Peyton while maintaining a solemn expression.

She handed Peyton the PP she had used the previous night and a bottle of lube, saying, "You have enjoyed me so far, but I have only scratched the surface of your rediscovery. I promised I would teach you more and so it begins; take this, go to the bathroom and put it in like I did last night, then come back." When Peyton turned around, Mary had her outfit ready for her: a plain white cotton thong, a tight shirt with spaghetti straps, a short flared skirt, and esparto wedges. Peyton gasped but walked away silently. She changed into a short, off-the-shoulder black minidress and black stiletto sandals while she waited for Mary. They exited the

structure and departed in an open Jeep that belonged to Mary. Peyton hung on tightly as it bounced out of the garage and traveled along the bumpy suburban roads.

The PP kept being forced into her ass by the bouncing; the sensation was not altogether unpleasant, and she felt her pussy getting wetter by the minute, her nipples becoming harder and harder. Peyton believed Mary purposefully used "B" roads for the entire hour she was driving to ensure the Jeep bounced as much as possible. The largest shopping complex in the city, Central World Bangkok, was their final destination. Mary gave Peyton a sweet kiss and talked softly to her as they exited the Jeep at the lowest parking level in the depths of the earth.

Peyton nodded as they boarded the elevator and headed up to the mall. "My little butterfly, follow my every order in the mall, do everything I say, it is part of what I want you to learn."

Mary knew where they were headed and led the way, leading them directly to a sizable sex shop in a far-off corner as they exited the lift and proceeded straight through the mall. Outside the store, she came to a stop and turned to Peyton.

"Now pay close attention; I want you to enter and remain inside until you have purchased a leather strap, a butt plug, and a pair of nipple clamps. I'll be in the store and might even approach you, but you won't even acknowledge me; to everyone else, you don't know who I am. Peyton was resolved not to let her buddy down; after all, how difficult could it be to purchase three things? "Good

luck little one, oh and hand over your mobile phone, you won't be needing it." She had no idea...

She entered with assurance and soon saw herself in a rack full of dildos, butt plugs, harnesses, clamps, belts, and straps—everything one could possibly want and more. She wandered through the shop gawking at everything that was on display, eventually coming to a counter and searching for a store employee. A tall young woman with blonde hair pulled back into a ponytail and wearing tight black trousers and a leather waistcoat appeared. She had the most unattainable heels on her feet. As the assistant saw Peyton speaking now, she raised an eyebrow.

Errr, I-I need a pair of nipple clamps, please, the blonde said as she turned to face Peyton.

"What do they serve? Do they suit you? Would you prefer clover clamps? the spring clamps? nut clamps? Let's see, pull your top up, and show me your tits,' Peyton said, stepping back in shock.

'Nooo! And why should I? Just a pair of clamps, please! The blonde spoke severely as she stood up:

You want to get clamps, so look here. It's my responsibility to make sure you get just what you need; otherwise, your beloved won't be too pleased with you, is she? Because, after all, it IS a she. Now remove the top and lean on this counter! After saying that, the blonde busied herself with removing a variety of clamps from a drawer. Peyton, who couldn't believe she was doing it, pulled her top up and exposed her tits in the meantime.

CHAPTER 11

Blondie applied a clover clamp to one of Peyton's nipples while pulling on it; Peyton didn't seem to notice much, so Blondie withdrew it. She next tried on a screw clamp, tightening it just enough to prevent it from falling. Despite Peyton's gasps, Blondie continued to tighten. They lost their grip, so Blondie threw those away as well. After that, she grabbed a pair of ominous-looking alligator clips with screw adjustments, opened one of them, and placed it on Peyton's nipple. Peyton took a sharp breath, and her nostrils flared as Blondie unfastened the adjustment, causing the clamps to close and bite the nipple with their sharp steel teeth. These clamps were a serious pair. Blondie didn't relax until she noticed that Peyton's eyes were beginning to well up with tears. On Peyton's other breast, she now performed the exercise once more.

She pulled out a few chains from under the counter and selected a chromed link chain, hooking it to both clamps and letting the chain hang blow Peyton's tits. "I think these clamps need a leash so your beloved can lead you about the room," she said. "What else did you want to get now that we have the clamps worked out?" Peyton flinched, expecting Blondie to loosen the clamps, but it was clear that wasn't going to happen, so she spoke.

Blondie grinned and walked away, saying, "Umm, I also need a leather strap, and a butt plug."

"Well, come on, I don't have all day, the straps are here, follow me," Peyton said, glancing after her.

But, everyone will see if I walk like this. Please! By this point, other customers were starting to notice the activity at this end of the store. A small crowd had formed to watch, with Mary among them as he pretended to be a regular customer. They watched as Blondie confronted Peyton aggressively.

"Now listen to this young woman, you come to my business to buy. I need to make sure that your lover is happy with your purchases. I need to make sure that you get exactly what she wants for you.

Blondie pulled her toward a counter a ways further down the shop by grasping the chain holding the nip clamps. Peyton asked as she stood there, "So what kind of strap are we looking for? I'm assuming you want 18 inches, 24 inches, or something in between. Do you like a single or double thickness? Leaning forward on the counter, I'll be the judge.

Blondie rolled her skirt up and slipped her thong down to her ankles, and Peyton leaned forward and gasped. As Blondie noticed the PP in her asshole, she heard her hold her breath. Her ass gaped as it emerged, and she felt as it was gently withdrew. Blondie came over and grabbed a couple straps and tawses from behind the counter. After some consideration, she decided on the 18inch, 2inch wide double thickness model. As she followed Peyton, there was a moment of silence followed by a movement and an ass-on-fire sensation. She screamed. Blondie swiftly stroked her six different buttocks. Peyton's shouts were more like yelps that came

in quick succession. Blondie paused, and Peyton recognized the voice:

It was Mary who said, "I think the 12inch single thickness may also make an impression on her, we could try that." Blondie nodded her agreement and instructed her to try on Peyton with any strap she chose. The throng that had been watching from a distance moved closer and cheerily gazed on as Mary stood behind Peyton, who whimpered softly in anticipation, and laid on six alternate strokes with the shorter strap.

As the two tormentors watched, appreciating their job, Peyton leaned forward, sobbing quietly with tears streaming from her nose. The shorter, narrower strap had deeper, more vibrant red marks, and it was clear to see how it differed from the longer, wider strap, which had wide, dark pink patches that were hot to the touch. They exchanged words for a bit before nodding. Blondie put the shorter strap aside and the longer one on the counter before speaking,

I recall you said you also required a butt plug, and with an ass like yours, I think I have just the model to fit.' With that, she rummaged among the drawers and produced a short, thick plug, black as coal and resembling a very fat cock, with well-defined veins and a large cock-head. Oval in shape, the flared base made it pleasant to wear underneath garments. Blondie allowed Peyton to have a brief glance at it, perhaps solely for the fun of observing Peyton's terrified expression and saucer-shaped eyes. Just take off your thong, push back your ass, and relax, my dear.

Peyton attempted to unwind, but she struggled since her heart was pounding like a tattooed drum. As fingers reaming in and out made her rear sticky, she felt them smearing lubrication in her asshole. Blondie continued to apply pressure after the fingers stopped moving, and the plug gradually slid into the hole a little at a time. As it inched closer, unabated and persistent, Peyton grunted. Blondie stopped when the sphincter muscles resisted the plug and allowed Peyton to gather herself. Before the second assault, which started after thirty seconds, the plug was again pushed in. This time, it subtly caused the sphincter to open up, and millimeter by millimeter, the silicone cockhead worked its way past the muscle ring. Unexpectedly, the head was past the sphincter when it smoothly went in till the muscle rested on the tiny area behind the skull. Blondie rose up after getting what she wanted, embarrassing Peyton as the audience applauded.

Blondie said, "It's as I thought, that plug is perfect for you; your lover will be very happy with your purchases. I'll pack it all up, you can pay, and then you can go. Oh, and since the plug fits you so well it would be a shame to remove it so you can wear it home."

Peyton squealed and started crying as the blood began to flow back into her nipples because they had been on for so long. After quickly packing and paying for her things, Peyton turned to depart but failed to spot Mary.

Peyton was standing by herself at the store's entrance, tears streaming down her face. She was far from home, her only friend was nowhere to be found, and because she didn't have a cell

phone, she was completely cut off from society. As Blondie emerged from the store and approached her, she had been standing there for 30 minutes and was preparing to look for someone to aid her.

She pointed to the back of the store where a small chamber was concealed behind a disguised door and said, "Hey you, slut, come here you have a phone call in my office." She picked up the phone from its cradle in the room and called Mary.

"Well done, my little butterfly. You have done well, followed every directive, and behaved in the manner in which I instructed you. Now you will return home with the blonde sex shop assistant. She is Swedish, and her name is Inga, but you will always address her as Miss." With that, she hung up the phone, and Peyton did the same. Peyton was beckoned to follow Inga as she picked up her handbag and rucksack after tidying up her makeup and was now prepared to leave. The two girls exited the store and made their way to the elevators. Inga shoved Peyton up against the wall and almost mauled her, kissing her and stroking her ample breasts. Peyton was clearly aroused but chose not to reciprocate. A low-slung sports car was parked in the back of the parking level where Peyton found herself after the elevator abruptly quit working. As soon as they arrived there, Inga told Peyton to lie down forward on the car's hood while she raised her skirt and removed a small leather paddle from her bag. Peyton's upper thighs and lower buttocks were the first places Inga began to pound her methodically. Peyton cried out in agony.

CHAPTER 12

"These ones are only for me," he said. "You sobbed when I beat you, you took the plug without crying too much, you didn't kiss me in the elevator, and you are too beautiful. But mostly, you are not mine; you belong to my friend, and I am merely helping to mistreat you, damn!"

Peyton shouted out more, her tears streamed from her eyes, and she was a blubbering mess by the time Inga finished thrashing her after ten minutes of non-stop beating. Her lower buttocks and thighs were a lovely deep red color that matched the thick stripes on the rest of the arse.

Inga instructed Peyton to enter the vehicle, but to pull up her skirt so that her naked bottom was on the leather seat; the cushion pushed the enormous butt plug farther in. Peyton saw how much time had passed as they pulled out of the mall parking lot and realized it was already early afternoon. They headed back to Mary's bungalow as they exited the suburbs. They needed to eat, so Inga stopped at a wayside eatery along the way. She urged Peyton to follow her to the bar, where she sat down on one of the tall stools. The poor girl carefully got onto the stool, taking care not to expose herself because her skirt was too short and her plug too evident.

Some of the other customers turned to look at the two; Peyton caught their attention with her short skirt and tight blouse, which revealed her bare nipples, and Inga caught their attention with her striking blonde hair and long legs, which revealed her

Scandinavian origin. For the two, Inga ordered hamburgers, fries, a side salad, and diet cokes. After eating in silence, Inga finished her meal and asked to use the restroom. She tapped Peyton on the arm to follow her. A large African-American who had been staring at them was inadvertently acknowledged by Inga as she turned to face him.

As soon as they arrived at the restrooms, which were located in the back, the man caught up with them. As the man joined them, Inga hurriedly escorted Peyton into the cubicle for people with disabilities. She was going to say anything when Inga gave her a strong slap, which caused her to cry.

"Don't even consider making a sound; your task is to amuse this man, who will choose whether you deserve to have the strap-on used by Mary, myself, or his cock to remove your anal cherry. Now get on your knees, slut, and work hard! '

Peyton sobbed softly as she fell to her knees; in the meantime, the man had unzipped his pants, revealing a massive circumcised cock that came out like a rigid spring. Peyton had never seen an erect cock before, thanks in large part to Fred, who had failed to deliver on two occasions. Peyton had never seen a cock this size; it was enormous, not really black but more of a really dark purple, and it seemed to throb, almost to pulse. Peyton had only ever seen cocks this size in the movies she had been watching on Fred's laptop. She made a "O" with her mouth and carefully grasped the cock with two hands as she delicately glided her lips over it, slowly over the cock, an inch at a time, up the shaft she went, trying to

recall what Mary had shown her. This was her first and only blow job since Fred's death. When the cock struck the back of her throat, she halted, slid out gently once again, and licked the head's underside as it came back to her lips. She did this frequently, inhaling deeply and licking her lips as she did so. She could hear the man groaning and murmuring.

"Yeah, child, yes... Use your tongue more, lick more vigorously—God, you're good, baby! He continued to encourage Peyton as she licked and sucked the enormous black cock. Peyton grasped his balls with her hands and began to delicately twist and massage them, which caused him to scream louder. Inga said.

"You like this, Zeke?" Remember, there's no pressure; it's up to you whether you take her anal cherry or we do.' Zeke nodded and pushed his massive cock more into Peyton's mouth. Peyton herself was shocked at how well she had taken that after relaxing her neck muscles, which allowed it to just slide into the back. Zeke backed away, and she held his cock steady while kissing and licking it all over, playing her tongue under it, sucking his balls one by one into her mouth, and then putting the cock back into her mouth and frantically bobbing her head on it. Ezekiel struggled and moaned as Peyton used her brand-new skills on him.

Peyton noticed a tremor developing in Zeke's cock slowly. She slowed down until the tremor stopped, at which point she picked up the beat once more. She continued to do this for a bit, getting her cues from the tremors and Zeke's groans. When Zeke pulled away, picked her up, spun her around, and shoved her up against

the sink, she had every intention of going for the gold. She had her own lubricant in her pussy, which he poked with two fingers. As some of it began to drip down her thighs, he peered down and noticed the flared base of the black butt plug. Peyton bit her teeth as the thick, cock-shaped lump of silicone slowly came out of her ass as he grinned as he grabbed hold of the base and dragged it out using a corkscrew motion. Ezekiel took advantage of the big opening in her asshole to insert his enormous cock into her eager hole. He still found it difficult and had to push himself quite hard even with the wide opening. Not only was his cock long, but it was also incredibly thick.

Peyton was in tears during this workout, but she didn't say anything as Zeke rammed his member into her ass. Zeke was taking her anal cherry at his own pace and on to his own terms.

Her tits, her breasts, and her nipples were all the focus of his hands as they encircled her. She squealed when he turned, and Inga had to correct her by threatening to beat her severely in the bathroom if she didn't stop. Peyton had to put up with it even though it got the desired outcome. She could see Inga in the mirror playing with her nips and pussy while Zeke reamed Peyton's ass while she was leaning against the restroom door with her waistcoat and fly zipper open. She felt Zeke's cock jerk in her ass as he was already getting close to the edge; he slowed down but the jerks persisted. Peyton felt as like her ass was on fire as he pounded harder and faster.

Peyton felt her own orgasm start to develop suddenly and abruptly. As a tremor ran through her pussy, she felt Zeke give her

one last yank in the ass, and she could feel his hot jism filling her asshole as she repeatedly came. She had no doubt that he had stolen her cherry, and she had cherished every second of it. He backed out and collapsed exhausted. A voice rang out from behind them,

It's my time now, I think. Would anyone like to kill me off? Inga smirked sheepishly as she stood there.

Peyton got to her feet and motioned for Inga to approach. She grabbed hold of her and gave her a passionate kiss before dropping her hands to touch Inga's exposed tits, which she enjoyed groping. They had swollen nipples that made them all the more attractive; Peyton toyed with them and with the thick nipples, she bent her head and sucked and licked them. They were not too big and stuck out proudly. Ezekiel had been fingering Inga in the meantime. He pushed his fingers in and out while flicking her clitoris with his other thumb, penetrating her pussy. It didn't take long for Inga to orgasm with ecstatic yells because she had already been on the verge of cumming. She was worn out and slumped back against the sink.

The three of them hurriedly cleaned themselves and exited the restroom. The girls went to their car, while Zeke climbed onto a Harley parked in front. Zeke followed them as they made their way back to Mary's bungalow after leaving the diner's parking lot. They arrived and discovered the Jeep and another Harley parked in front. Zeke and Inga parked next to them, got out of their cars, and entered the bungalow.

CHAPTER 13

Mary was drinking white wine in the living room when they arrived, and the man Peyton had seen in the dungeon the second night she had spent there was sitting on the opposite sofa. He sat drinking a beer and appeared at ease. She was decked out in a brief pair of shorts, a breast tube, high-heeled sandals, and a bun, while he was dressed in leather pants, a white T-shirt, and biker boots. "Now that you two are here, we can play some more games," they said. As she said so, she stood up and led the way to the dungeon, stopping in an open space when the ladies and the gentlemen were ready to proceed downstairs. They turned to face the other three after she said, "Peyton, come and stand here with me. I want to present you to these great individuals." Peyton, you have already met Inga, Zeke, our manly Texan friend, and yesterday you met Arnold, a longtime friend who is Austrian and will cheerfully take cock as well as give it. When they were being introduced, there was a muted ripple of laughter, and Peyton grinned at them. Peyton, in just two days, you have picked up a lot of knowledge. According to what Inga has informed me, you dealt Zeke an even better blow than you did to Arnold. You took my fingers to take your virginity and my strap-on excellently, and you learnt how to walk with a Princess Plug and a Butt Plug. Zeke recently stole your anal virginity, which, based on what I've heard, you appeared to appreciate. You still have a lot to learn, but the next thing you need to do is have a man fuck you so that your pussy has a real cock inside of it.

Despite the fact that Peyton had already had a variety of sex acts, been offered many delights, and even had a flogger and a strap used on her, she had yet to experience a real flesh-and-blood cock. Tonight might well be the night, based on what she had just heard. All three women sat down on the enormous bed in the dungeon after being escorted there by Ingaand Mary. They then began softly kissing Peyton all over her body. While Mary sat on her and began to aggressively eat her pussy, Inga focused on her stunning breasts. Peyton's nipples were becoming extremely wet and rock-hard. Inga took each one in her lips and sucked deeply while carefully biting down; this made Peyton furious. Peyton groaned more as a result of Inga's flicking of her large nipples. Mary slipped two fingers into Peyton's extremely wet pussy with ease. She then took some of the juice and smeared it on Peyton's rim before using her other hand to slide two, then three, fingers into Peyton's asshole.

While Zeke and Arnold prepared for Peyton's next educational phase, this continued for a while. Arnold had stripped down, wrapped a cock ring around the base of his cock and balls, and inserted a large butt plug deep inside his ass. As a result, he was sporting a massive, purple cock that was fully engorged and ready for action. He gently stroked it. Zeke had also undressed, but he didn't need anything to maintain the hardness of his own enormous cock. They stopped what they were doing and pulled Peyton over, placing her on all fours. She was now kneeling while leaning forward on her hands and panting; her tits hung down invitingly.

They proceeded up to the bed where the girls were having fun. Mary spotted them coming and gestured to Inga. While the two men climbed on, the other two girls left the bed.

Arnold moved in front of her face while Zeke kneeled behind her. When they drew closer to her, Arnold began to rub his cock all over her face. Peyton opened her lips to take it in and gently licked the shaft's underside. She kept sucking and licking it while keeping her eyes closed as he gently pushed it in. As the females applied more lubrication to her hole, she felt fingers on her ass. After that, the touching stopped, and she felt someone poking and pushing her at the door. As Zeke pressed his cock into her hole, she let go of her sphincter muscles. She froze in fear and sealed her hole because it seemed so big. All that happened was that Inga violently squeezed her nipples when she realized what had transpired. Her nipples were placed in a pair of tight alligator clamps, and a chain was linked to them and wound around her back. Zeke could now pull on her nipples if he wanted to! She cried even through Arnold's cock because of the way he pulled, which badly stretched her nipples and caused her tits to twist to the side.

Zeke's cock resumed its inch-by-inch ascent into Peyton's asshole as she opened her sphincter, moving slowly but methodically. Peyton's ass appeared to soften and take the invader more comfortably with each inch that Zeke halted, allowing them both to catch their breath. It took more than 10 minutes to insert the entire eight-inch-thick cock into her tunnel, but once it did, the

balls began to hit her pussy. As he held Peyton by her sides, Zeke let go. He kept her immobile.

Peyton on a spit roast with Zeke's cock buried in her ass and Arnold's cock buried in her mouth looked like a painting. The three were completely still, and nothing moved the scene until a flash and a click were noticed. 'For posterity,' asserted Mary, 'for her album,' 'for her collection,' and 'for my memories,' respectively. The three on the bed then slowly began to perform; Zeke gradually withdrew, Arnold did likewise, and then they both pushed in. slowly to start. Over time, this motion was repeated, with the only variation being that as time went on, the thrusts grew angrier and angrier. Peyton looked to be getting more upset because she started making tiny yelps and gasps of pleasure or pain.

She struggled to hold back her gag reflex as Arnold repeatedly hit the back of her throat in her mouth. Arnold totally opened up his cock and let Peyton to kiss and suck his bell-end before pushing back in with his balls hard and purple and full of come that was itching to burst. Inga rubbed his balls while rhythmically thrusting them. Each thrust was followed by a squeeze from Inga, which caused his face to twist into a grimace.

Ezekiel was currently pounding into her ass in a frantic manner, his balls slapping against her wet, engorged, and hungry pussy. Mary seized Zeke's balls and squeezed them rhythmically while holding them in a vice-like grasp.

CHAPTER 14

He grunted as he propelled, wanting more and more to stuff his thick come into Peyton's asshole. Peyton squealed each time he re-entered her hole as he repeatedly pulled out completely before thrusting back in.

Mary and Inga were having a blast as the three of them gradually came to their climax. Although they were aware that their turn would come later, their immediate goal was to ensure that the three people on the bed came together. Zeke and Arnold were well on their way to a climax and would be cumming any minute now, nothing could stop them, but Peyton seemed to be waning and they wanted to get her back on track. They released the balls they were squeezing and climbed off the bed.

Inga made the decision to give Peyton's pussy some attention because it had gone unattended and unfilled for so long. She lubricated her fingers before placing her hand beneath the American's body, moved it up to the pussy, where she discovered the clitoris, which was stiff and engorged. She began rubbing it in time with Zeke and Arnold's thrusts. Not only did this have a magical impact on Peyton, who began to tremble and shake, but also on Zeke, who felt these vibrations flowing through her pussy. He continued to thrust, rocking Peyton onto Arnold's cock and gently bringing him to the brink of his climax.

Arnold's cock suddenly spasmed to the point of ecstasy, and hot jism spurted out, filling Peyton's mouth. Arnold's balls appeared to suddenly contract. Ezekiel then dumped his testicles into

Peyton's accommodating ass as she cried out inaudibly while her pussy pulsated with pleasure as a result of this. They combined into a single, writhing mass that was emitted heat and the fragrance of climactic corpses. Zeke and Arnold each pulled their individual cocks out of Peyton's holes as they collapsed. They were all happy together. Mary and Inga grinned at the tableau before turning to leave.

The dungeon bed was large enough for the three to sleep soundly there throughout the night, so Inga and Mary left them there. They went up to Mary's bungalow, poured themselves a drink, and then carried it into the bedroom where they undressed, turned on some mellow jazz, and relaxed on the bed.

Inga Ekström, a typical Swedish girl who was only twenty-two and had lived in Bangkok for three years, was nearly six feet tall, with long blonde hair, and perky tits. Fred had invited her and her girlfriend to come on vacation when he offered to hire them both as models for his film studios. The two females had agreed to participate and had been in a few movies, but when Fred wanted to move them onto the heavier material, her partner thought it was too much and fled to Sweden. On the other hand, Inga stayed because she liked the way of life. She first met Mary during her brief modeling career, and they became more than just friends throughout their year-long residence in this home as lovers. Inga stopped her film career at this point and began working in the sex business, a position Mary had secured for her. She had been working in the shop for two years when she became the store

manager. Inga enjoyed her life in Bangkok since she was independent, had three cats, lived in a wonderful apartment, had a respectable salary at her job, and was not at all like her controlling and overbearing stepmother. Her thoughts were thousands of miles away and a few years ago as she laid in bed.

away one night in a car accident caused by a drunk driver, which was tragic, but made worse when one learned that she was the drunk driver and had killed four other people when her Volvo crashed into a small Fiat carrying two young couples returning from a concert. Mrs. Mrtenson, whose first name Inga could never pronounce as Ewa, served as her father's advocate as he sorted through legal documents for many hours each day. She was well aware of April's drinking issue because she knew the family.

From the moment Mrs. Mrtenson wed her father, the tone was set. She appeared to believe Inga was too much like her mother and wanted to stifle any type of independent thought or desire to have fun. No celebrations, no laughter, no enjoyment, and frequent consequences for crossing the line. The strap, the belt, the cane, and the riding crop have all been used on Inga's behind since she was 10 years old. Between the ages of six and ten, hand spankings over Mrs. Mrtenson's knee were employed as punishment.

Mrs. Mrtenson controlled every aspect of Inga's life with an iron fist. She made all of her clothing, food, drink, books, and travel arrangements. Although her father never found anything wrong with his new wife and always gave her the benefit of the doubt, Inga frequently sobbed herself to sleep and was unable to confide in him.

Agnese began to visit her home more frequently, and they would listen to music or do homework together. Inga would visit her home for the same purpose; Mrs. Mrtenson had never permitted sleepovers. The girls would frequently skip school to spend the

day playing with each other behind some bushes in the park or the woods. Every time they were together, their passion intensified and threatened to overtake them like an express train. Nobody knew about their small affair because they were so discreet about it and didn't inform any of their friends or family.

Or so they believed.

One summer day, Mrs. Mrtenson was waiting for Inga in her bedroom when she got home from school. Inga was about to start speaking when she received an enormous slap that knocked her to the ground. Before she could gather herself, her shorts and pants were being pulled down, and she was being pushed onto her desk. The strikes then started. There was no pause as the strap was being used on her arse in a way that had never been done before. The thick strap Mrs. Mrtenson, who she knew the old hag had ordered online from Scotland, used to repeatedly strike her all over the back, from the center of the buttocks to the back of her knees. She cried, "Stop!" as her pleadings and tears went unheard. Please! ", ', 'Why? nevertheless, in vain. After 45 minutes, it finally came to an end.

Mrs. Mrtenson spoke softly,

You are a warped product of bad genes and contemporary civilization, much like your mother, who has bad genes! How do you thank me for trying to raise you to be a well-behaved, obedient, and conforming child ever since I wed your poor suffering father? by behaving in a lesbian harlot manner!

CHAPTER 15

I have learned that you have been engaging in some type of "relationship" with the Larsson girl, whose name is Agnese, I believe. They have decided to send the girl to boarding school in England, which should take care of her soon enough as they still uphold severe discipline unlike the namby-pamby schools here in Scandinavia. I just spent an hour on the phone with her sad mother. You, young woman, I will beat this small fancy out of your body by beating your bottom with the strap for 30 minutes every morning and 30 minutes every evening before you go to bed. You won't be attending school anymore because I've hired a private tutor. She's Scotch, 65 years old, and quite rigorous. I should also mention that she has your father's and my permission to cane and strap you as she sees fit. You still have tonight's strapping to do when you go to bed, so get out of the room and take a shower.

Inga was sobbing as she thought back to that time in her life, a time when she endured daily beatings, was forbidden from seeing her friends, and was also forbidden from going to her friends' homes. This carried on for easily a whole year, her breakfast was always thirty minutes of the strap, some days a two-tailed tawse, some days a three-tailed, sometimes a plain strap, then off to the study room with the dour faced Mrs Anchali who always found cause to punish Inga, she loved to have the girl lift her skirt and lower her panties, then to lean on the desk as she would invariably deliver fifty strokes of her two-tailed tawse followed by six of the

cane. Up until tea time, when the instructor would leave, lessons would continue. Inga would complete whatever homework that was left for her after supper until night, which was always around 10:30 when Mrs. Mrtenson would give her her bedtime strapping. Inga recalled how delighted she was when her father told her that Mrs. Anchali had suffered a severe stroke and would no longer be able to tutor her, and that she would now be sent to a private school. There, she met Boden native Margareta, and they fell in love. This was the companion who had gone to Thailand with Inga and who had entered and exited her life with equal ease.

Mary turned to face Inga when she saw her crying and gave her a gentle kiss on the cheek and eyelid. Inga continued to sob as Mary rocked her and held her tight, but eventually she stopped and gave Mary a hug as well. Mary determined that this would be an excellent opportunity for them to enjoy themselves privately.

Being still aroused after the dungeon experience, the two women locked lips passionately and soon had drenched pussies and stiffly engorged nipples. Inga was pushed back against the pillow by Mary, who then sat on top of her and massaged Inga's completely shaved slit with her trimmed pussy. She experienced a jolt that extended all the way to her toes. Inga reached up, fondled Mary's tits and tweaked her nipples before holding them tightly between her thumb and forefinger while simultaneously pulling them out. Mary leaned forward and gasped with delight as she enjoyed having her tits and nipples tightly squeezed. In order to give Mary

a long, passionate kiss and to caress her back, Inga dragged her down onto her. She then used her long nails to scratch the area.

They all rolled to the side together. Mary moved her fingers down Inga's body, ending at her pubic area. There, she delicately scratched Inga all around her mound and slit while recalling how much she adored the Scandinavians' shaved slits. After giving it a slow, sensual kiss and sucking each labia in turn, she spun around and began stabbing the slit with her tongue by pushing it in and moving it up and down its length. She located the clit, which was fatty and engorged, and flicked it with her sharp tongue. The more she flicked it, the slicker it became. Mary gently bit into the clit with her teeth, which caused Inga to scream. Mary grinned inside because she enjoyed hearing Inga react in this way.

After repeatedly licking, sucking, flicking, and stabbing her pussy, she united her fingers and tongue to move them up and down the slit. Two fingers entered Inga's hole first, slowly pushing their way in and then slowly pulling themselves out, in and out, in and out, faster and faster like a piston. As Inga's breathing got louder, a third finger soon joined the previous two. Nevertheless, nothing compared to the gasps and cries that could be heard when a fourth finger was inserted. When Mary started using her thumb on Inga's clit, she was already working her fingers in and out of Inga's pussy hole. The thumb and tongue were then alternated to thrill the stiff, engorged, and deep purple clitoris.

With her hands supporting Mary's head, Inga massaged the Asian's scalp while twirling her fingers through his hair. Inga

gasped as Mary's middle finger broke the plane of the sphincter and plunged into the hot rectum while using her free hand to collect sticky pussy juice from the Swedish woman's tight small asshole. With her eyes clamped tight and her head slowly rocking side to side, Inga let out a silent scream.

The buzz began in the pit of her stomach and moved up to her nipples before she felt the burning in her ears as her climax approached gradually but certainly. The sensation suddenly hit her in her clitoris and pussy hole like an express train. Inga was a squirter, and Mary knew it. She utilized it to her own delight, and she loved to savor Inga's juice as she came over and again. Mary continued the finger-fucking while pressing on Inga's engorged g-spot.

Inga clearly remembered the first time she had done it and still felt the same joy as she drew Mary up to her face and kissed her deeply while savoring her own juices. She then seized Mary's nipples and licked them until they were rock hard. Reaching over to the bedside table, she took two spring clamps that she had prepared earlier in the day and attached them together with a leash. Inga took Mary's erect nipples and clamped them with the two painful objects while enjoying his cries of pain. As the nipples appeared to get fatter, she kissed her partner's mouth to calm her down and inserted her tongue deeply into the other's mouth.

As she continued to slowly pull on the leash, causing Mary to struggle and wail in anguish, she reached down with one hand and massaged his genitalia.

CHAPTER 16

Inga stretched the nipples out impossibly by pulling on the leash more firmly the louder the cries became. Inga had to decide whether to push Mary over the brink right away or to wait until she was closer to her climax because they had the entire night to enjoy themselves.

Inga's decision was greatly aided by Mary's pleading with her to allow her to climax, which allowed her cruel side to manifest itself once more.

'NO! I'm going to spread out your pleasure by making it painful, and if I decide to be kind to you, maybe I'll even allow you have a climax tonight.

Saying this, Inga grabbed a pair of shackles from the nightstand, handcuffed Mary's hands together, hauled them up over her head, and attached them to a secret small chain hanging from the headboard. Inga trembled in frustration, her tears a sign of her annoyance. She tried to negotiate after first pleading, protesting, and negotiating, but all that got her was a twin penis gag shoved into her mouth and buckled tight. In addition to the six inches of considerably thicker black cock sticking straight up from her mouth, Mary now had a short, thick rubber cock in her mouth.

Inga spun around and deftly lowered her oily, sticky pussy over the dildo that was massively protruding from Mary's mouth, pulling on the leash attached to the Asian's tits as she did so. She appeared to be riding a thoroughbred in a race as she did this. She pulled the tits up as hard as she could as Mary writhed beneath

her, screamed through the gigantic cock gag, and fucked herself on the big black cock.

Inga released the leash, slid forward onto Mary's body, and positioned herself so that her face was directly over the latter's dripping-wet pussy hole, which she licked and sucked on for some time. Mary squirmed under Inga as a result, which just made Inga more ecstatic as she was quickly approaching her second orgasm thanks to the penis gag. Mary muffled a scream as Inga added more clamps to her delicate labia, which only served to pique her interest. Inga fucked herself on the black silicone while devouring Mary's clit and pussy like crazy.

Inga grabbed the leash firmly and pushed while stretching the labia out. There was a sizable wet mark on the bed and the pussy was now pouring. Mary's labia were constantly tense since Inga attached the leash to another chain at the foot of the bed. After doing this, she took a vibrating wand and ran it up and down Mary's slit while lowering the intensity and purposefully missing the clit. She repeated this a few times till she felt Mary writhing beneath her; she was so near to going into orgasm that it was getting difficult to restrain herself.

Inga climbed off Mary and knelt next to her. She grabbed the leash from the nipple clamps and attached it to a long chain at the headboard. At this point, Mary was being cruelly forced to have her labia pulled down and her tits dragged up by alligator clamps with steel tips. The muffled cries, as well as the writhing and jumping, persisted as Inga continued to play the wand on Mary's

clit and slit; sooner or later, she reasoned, this had to come to a stop.

Although Inga wanted to repeat herself, the emotion she was experiencing was too good to waste. The Asian thought this was the end and she would not get the chance to have a climax, and she was crying tears of sadness just as Inga came explosively, once more squirting all over her lover. The sight on the Asian's face was priceless.

When Inga placed the wand firmly to the trim Thai pussy, Mary probably believed this was the end of it for her. Nevertheless, it only lasted for a minute before Mary arched her back as far away from the terrible as she could and cried out through the gag as her climax hit her like a truck. She arrived in waves, bouncing on the bed simultaneously. Once it was over, Inga took away the wand, took away Mary's penis gag, but left her chained to the bed, demonstrating to her the affection these girls felt for one another as she kissed and hugged her.

Inga embraced Mary, whom she had left handcuffed to the bed, and the two quickly drifted off to sleep.

The five were dead asleep when the phone rang in the morning. Only Inga, who was upstairs, was able to get up. Mary tried to get up but realized she was still restrained to the bed, so she signalled to Inga to free her. As she answered the phone, Inga scolded the caller.

'Hi! Oh, it's you Larry, Mary couldn't come to the phone right now since she's really busy. What can I do to help? The others are all

there, so ten o'clock would be a fantastic time. She hung up and said to Mary, "That was Larry; he's coming at 10; will he be the one stealing Peyton's cherry?" If he is, the lucky girl! '

Larry was an American bodybuilder, about seven feet tall, with a cock to be proud of and a body that measured nine inches of pure pleasure. He had been the star of several of Fred's films, but he had come to the conclusion that he could earn more money by acting as a stud-for-hire for various pornographic film studios. During his early days with Fred, he made friends with Mary, Inga, and the others and continued to do so both in and out of bed.

Larry was a versatile player who was known to bat for both sexes. He was equally at ease penetrating a pussy as he was an ass, and he was equally at ease taking a blow job as he was giving one. Larry was truly a man for all occasions. Peyton had already had her mouth and ass taken, she had been entered with a strap-on, but a cock had never been up her snatch; Mary had already made arrangements for him to come and take her actual virginity; Larry would have the honor.

Inga released Mary since they had work to do, but not before giving the Asian a strong kiss and bite on the nipples till the latter started crying. They had a shower together but didn't have time to play, so after drying off, they put on a thong and a light summer dress, which would serve for now. To wake up the group, they descended the stairs.

Just as they were about to descend the basement stairs, they heard weird noises: dungeon groans and grunts.

CHAPTER 17

The two girls sped down to prevent the guys from stealing Peyton's cherry. Arnold posed no threat because he only fucked ladies on command and rather preferred to penetrate guys or be penetrated. Zeke, on the other hand, was a totally other beast and would do anything in a skirt!

Not too soon at all! On all fours, Peyton was naked, and he was about to stick his rabid prick in her hot pussy. STOPPPP! Mary and Inga both yelled. Zeke stood still and said, "You are NOT the one who will take her pussy cherry Zeke, someone else is on the way for that task; just her ass was yours to crack.

Peyton trembled and groaned as Ezekiel rubbed his cock against her tender lips before nodding and getting out of bed. She was one very aroused woman who only wanted to be penetrated once and for all. Peyton saw Mary and Inga before realizing that she would have to wait rather than pleading. The girls approached her in the meantime and urged her to get dressed and go upstairs while throwing her a thong and a summer dress similar to theirs.

They all went into the kitchen when the front door opened and there was Arnold with freshly baked croissants and crusty rolls for everyone; the guy knew you had to feed a body well if you wanted it to perform. Arnold was nowhere to be found so the four of them went upstairs to rustle up some breakfast before Larry came at ten. The five of them now sat down to enjoy some hot coffee and Arnold's contribution while conversing, sometimes it seemed, simultaneously. The females were dressed in breezy summer

dresses, which allowed glimpses of their thongs and nipples. The impact of this view on the males, who were wearing shorts and T-shirts, was pretty obvious.

When the door unexpectedly opened, the talk had already changed from benign and commonplace to slightly more risqué, and there was a chance they would wind up back on the bed. Peyton was enthralled by Larry when he stooped to enter and wore a tight muscle shirt and tight slacks that revealed a significant bulge. She had never seen a man like him before. Peyton was introduced to him by Mary.

Peyton sat there in shock, she knew eventually her pussy would be fucked by a real cock but had assumed it would be Zeke, never in her wildest dreams would she have imagined a macho muscle man like Larry would be her cock-man. Larry is six feet and nine inches tall with a nine inch cock to go with it. You will have the pleasure of being fucked by that cock in a little while, but first the two of you will entertain us.

The three girls moved down to the dungeon to get ready. Mary and Inga removed Peyton's dress, and they then restrained her hands with leather restraints connected by a short chain. They then attached the chain to a hook hanging from the ceiling, and Mary raised it with a remote control. Peyton's arms slowly rose, stretching as far as they could, and it stopped when she was on tiptoes. She was given a blindfold to wear while having a penis gag firmly strapped to her face and weighted spring clamps

connected to her nipples. The two girls took a step back to acknowledge their diligence.

Peyton was fearful and felt exposed. What would they do to her? In actual measurements, how large was a nine-inch cock? Would she be able to snort it down? on her tongue? in her behind? When she heard men's footsteps approaching, all these thoughts were going through her head. Oh my Goodness, she was about to face a difficult decision.

The weights were repeatedly held up and released as she felt them being played with; this aroused her and made her feel like her pussy was getting moist. Every time they were released, she felt a rush of pleasure pass through her, her pussy getting wetter, and she could feel her thong getting moist. It smelled and felt like leather as it was being trailed down her back and ass. She suddenly experienced the same over her breasts and down her stomach. She realized it had to be riding crops because they were toying with them on her body because it was rigid but leathery. She had never been this hot before as a result of this therapy; her thong felt drenched and her pussy fluid was now dripping down her thighs. Then came a halt.

She felt the crop hit her in the ass with a hiss, followed by a thump. She squirmed in her chains and tried to scream through the gag. She winced as she heard a second hiss. She heard a thump, but no pain, only another muffled scream. Who else was getting the crop, she wondered? The second victim received the fourth hiss and thump, while she received the third one on her ass, this time with

more agonizing pain. For some time, the sequence was repeated: hiss, thump, pain, grunt, hiss, thump, someone else's grunt. The area of her ass where the crop hurt the most was from the center hump down to the upper thigh. Once they had stopped, she began to cry and sob while hearing another person do the same. She dangled from the chain, worn out.

A short while later, she felt the crop being played on her nipples, round breasts, and tits. This also came to an abrupt end, and she felt fire on her nipples and breasts as the crop was used quickly and ruthlessly on her tits, paying particular attention to her nipples and underneath. Her legs gave way and she was left hanging from the chain, swinging while she was being struck raw. She screamed through the gag once again, and for good measure, a second person used a crop on her thighs down to the backs of her knees. She experienced the crop on her abdomen, front thighs, and even vaginal area during the session. She was unable to keep track of time, but soon it came to an end. Although she hurt and throbbed, she was also wet, alive, and heated.

When the blindfold was taken off, she could see Arnold standing a short distance away, chained up just like her and covered with crop markings down to his front and back knees. Like she did, he swung as he hung from the chain. She understood that all of her marks must be the same. It was now obvious who was utilizing the crops; Mary and Inga were standing next to her, while Zeke and Larry were standing with Arnold. Arnold was left chained while she was lifted off the ground and transported to a small bed

she had never seen before. They laid her on it with her head and legs hanging down on opposite sides. Her ankles were also chained to the bed, and they extended their arms out on either side of her. She waited in this posture while her severe cropping was still hurting her.

Ezekiel approached Peyton's head and gently put his large, black cock inside her mouth as she relaxed her muscles. He gently slid the cock back out once it had touched the back of her throat. He came to a stop, leaving only the head in her mouth, which she licked like an ice cream cone before slowly sliding back in.

When she couldn't see, someone was toying with her pussy and massaging her clit and labia with something firm and moist. Even with the large cock in her mouth, she sighed in satisfaction. When a second tongue joined the first, she realized it had to be a tongue because it was too flexible and wet to be anything else. It was uncomfortable to feel two tongues playing on her slit and clit.

She was loving it and wanted to be fucked. All this movement combined with the recent cropping had made her the wettest she had ever been. a real, hard cock was used, not a rubber fake. The tongues on her pussy persisted, and now slim, long-nailed female hands were playing with her nipples. As the touch was too intimate and delicate to be a guy's, she assumed Mary and Inga were the lickers.

Where was Larry then? She questioned herself in this way.

Zeke removed his cock from her lips and twisted her head to the side while he talked so she could see.

CHAPTER 18

See, Peyton, Larry is getting ready for you, and before long, you'll get the whole cock!

When she turned to look, she saw that Larry's enormous cock was being greedily sucked by Arnold, who had been unhooked and was now kneeling with his wrists bound behind his back. Till he saw Peyton glancing at them, Larry steadily pushed it into and out of Arnold's hungry mouth. Then he stopped.

Peyton was able to see Larry's enormous member in all its splendor as he carefully removed it from Arnold's mouth. That most virgin of pusses is ready to be penetrated by nine thick, throbbing purple inches of cock. Peyton's mother had forewarned her that tampons were wicked and gave "impure" ideas to girls who used them. She described a pussy that had never experienced cock in its thirty years of life, a pussy that had never even had a tampon inserted. Mary and Inga had taken care of that for a pussy that had just recently experienced what it was like to be inside of anything. They had exposed the pussy to penetration with their fingers and the strap-on. Now Larry would introduce it to Master Cock's joys.

Zeke released her head's hold and allowed her to incline it so she could stare down as Larry walked away from Arnold and vanished from vision. She observed how Mary and Inga moved away from her but Larry remained seated at her knees. She felt something nudge her already wet pussy as he approached her cautiously. She

attempted to go forward, desperate to get past Larry, but this only made him retreat.

She unwound as Larry continued to massage up and down her slippery crack while poking her pussy. This time, she was unable to stop herself from edging forward and was furious when Larry pulled back again. Ezekiel took her by the ears and shoved his cock deep into her mouth before hitting the back of her throat, which nearly made her vomit. She understood the message this time and stopped creeping forward. Larry once again touched her pussy with his cock.

He first stroked it on her erect clit before rubbing it from top to bottom of her wet slit. Zeke's cock prevented her from making any louder noises than a muted groan as she made sad noises. Larry stopped stroking and silently pushed while cocking right up to Peyton's hole's entrance. It appeared to be stationary.

After that, it was in. When Peyton screamed, Zeke withdrew so that everyone could hear her.

She cried out for Larry to stop, moaned and whimpered when he finally did, and then begged him to continue. He pulled it out gently and stopped with just the head inside after pushing it all the way in till his balls caught her behind. She pleaded with him to force it upon her, to fill her up, and to hard fuck her. Larry did this. As her cries grew louder and louder, he fucked her harder and harder. They had finished with her cries when Zeke broke through her mouth once more. He gave her the same vicious mouth fuck

that Larry gave her pussy. The two men were really pummeling the American, and they hoped she would never forget it.

Mary and Inga approached the spit-roasted Peyton after occupying themselves with tormenting the bound Arnold and playing with each other's bodies. Mary lubricated her fingers before slipping her hand under the New Yorker's ass. She then slowly fucked the tight ass with the fingers, slowly in, out, in, out. With each thrust, the ass was loosened a little more, which was helpful for the plans they had for the upcoming days.

But, Inga leaned closer and began to lick and suck the American's extremely firm nipples. Peyton attempted to get her chest off the bed but was blocked by her shackles. She gripped the left nipple with her teeth and bit hard before pulling out as far as she could. She yelled out in anguish and cried freely as this was repeated with the right nipple. Inga persisted in doing this, stretching the nipples to a length of two inches and pulling the tits into impossibly long cones.

For a while, the assault persisted until Peyton was reduced to a trembling mass. Inga fastened a chain to her nipples with a set of clamps. She carefully raised herself up the chain, raising Peyton's tits into peaks. A vibrating butt plug was then put into Peyton's ass by Mary after she had pulled her fingers out. She turned it on to the medium position. Peyton trembled and shook; if not for two cocks penetrating her, she would have jumped off the bed. She changed the plug's pace and type of vibration by using a remote

control to speed it up and then slow it down. Peyton reacted by moaning, crying, and meowing.

Mary, who was essentially the "Mistress of Ceremonies," was watching for the indicators that the session was gradually coming to a head. She had spent the day before arranging it, had secured the attendance of the necessary players, and had made sure everything was in order. Since everything had so far gone as planned, the conclusion had to be the same.

They didn't want to push Peyton too far because she was already heavily perspiring and might pass out. They gave each other nods as a prearranged cue to slow down. Mary, Inga, and Zeke halted what they were doing, took off her straps, removed the butt-plug and clamps, and moved away. Only Larry carried on with his work. He went onto the bed and tightly held Peyton, who grabbed him in return and sobbed into his chest as he continued to pump into her pussy. Peyton was driven over the edge when his come continued to fill her pussy as he kept thrusting; she arrived in waves of gratification.

She gave Larry a delicate kiss before licking his somewhat limp cock. She kissed his mouth once more after rubbing her tongue all over his cock and balls. She had been well fucked, and she had enjoyed every second of it. The fact that Peyton had reached adulthood today, at the age of 30, was significant to Larry, who held her close and gave her a sweet kiss. But, it's never too late to experience first-time fucking!

CHAPTER 19

Mary grinned, another job well done. She would check the concealed cameras later, when no one was present, to make sure they had captured everything accurately.

Peyton needed time to process the tremendous screw she had just had, so Larry carefully carried her and placed her on the small bed. He kissed her and then left her to rest. She quickly nodded off after closing her eyes, weary.

While this was going on, Mary and Inga took center stage. They both got on the king-sized bed and started kissing and fondling each other. Inga was loving Mary's attention as the females knelt facing each other and touched tits as they kissed, and she fell back onto the bed when Mary abruptly shoved her roughly. When Zeke restrained her and chained her arms to the headboard's corners, she was going to stand up. She is now tightly spread-eagled.

She was now powerless when Larry helped chain her feet to the footboard's corners. Mary grinned at her and said, "Payback!" Inga opened her eyes wide because she knew Mary would punish her severely for the session the previous evening. She had kind of been hoping for this.

Mary approached Inga and pulled a medium leather flogger out of a drawer before slowly beating her on the thighs from the knees to the top, but not yet hitting the pussy. Inga groaned as the flogger slowly began to strike her tummy, not inflicting any pain. Mary climbed all the way to her chest, but she hasn't yet hit the tits. From the top down to the knees and back again, up and down, over and

over, the flogger returned to her thighs. This time, it was faster and harsher. When her breaths accelerated, Inga gritted her teeth. The flogger eventually ceased. She resumed breathing normally.
Mary grinned at her as she raised the flogger to her shoulder, brought it down again on her abdomen, and started tattooing her up to her tits without actually hitting them. Faster and harder than before, up and down. Inga moaned and bit her bottom lip, feeling the pain. When her breathing started to get labored and ragged, the flogger paused. Mary waited for Inga to start breathing normally once more. She grinned at her once again.
A smaller flogger with just four inches of shoelace-thin leather tails and a three-inch-thick handle was used in its place by Mary. She turned to face Inga's feet and delicately tapped her mound with the little flogger. The tails swooped down and struck her along the length of her pussy. Inga pursed her lips in response; it was satisfying. Mary performed the action repeatedly, accelerating and escalating the stroke with each repetition. The "Ooohs!" and "Aaaahs!" ' were hitting her mercilessly as they came thick and fast.
Inga began to beg her companion to stop at this point, but she was ignored. As the flogger struck the Swede's extremely moist pussy, squelching noises began to join the cries for help. As Mary suddenly stopped, she turned the whip around and forced the handle into Inga's extremely red and moist pussy as she was now pleading and sobbing nonstop. It slipped in, and Mary cautioned

her that there would be hell to pay if she let it to fall out. Inga firmly nodded.

Mary began hitting Inga's breasts with a 12-inch plastic ruler after plugging her pussy while avoiding the nipples. When Mary targeted Inga's nipples, her whimpers became into suppressed cries, which then evolved into frantic shouts of anguish and desperate cries for mercy. These two large, dense, and hardened purple protrusions on Inga's chest grew to be the center of attention for her buddy.

Mary put down the ruler and picked up her medium flogger once again. She beat Inga on her already-abused tits with it, each blow making the area redder. She continued to paint until she had a uniform shade of purple; this would take days to clear off, and she grinned in satisfaction. After viciously flogging the plugged pussy, she tossed the small flogger that had been inserted in Inga's pussy to the side and focused her attention back to the plugged pussy. As a result, she had a clearer target to work on for the next 10 minutes. She started by using the flogger across the pussy, then after five minutes, she switched positions and used it down the pussy, making sure the flogger's tail ends were striking Inga directly on her clit.

Inga had become nothing more than a sobbing, blubbering mess. Mary was inflicting absolute agony, the kind of agony she knew Inga adored and savored; if it grew intolerable, she knew the safeword would be screamed, and everything would stop—but it hadn't. Inga continued with confidence because she had actually

never used the safeword once in the entire time they had known one another.

Mary put down the flogger and grabbed a pair of nipple clamps—alligator clamps, to be precise—with sharp, serrated metal teeth. It was no easy task to wear these clamps. The tears started to pour again as she opened them and forcibly squeezed Inga's nipples with them. The Swedish let out a muffled cry. Mary connected the two clamps with a thin chain, lowered a hanging hook and connected the chain to it, and then elevated the chain once more, raising the tits high enough to form cones. In an unsuccessful attempt to get out of bed, Inga arched her back.

Mary placed a vibrating wand on Inga's pussy slit and ran it up and down to wet it while she was in this position. After thoroughly lubricating it, she placed it on her clit and turned it on "high," electrifying Inga, who let out a long "oooohh!" Mary held the wand there while seeing Inga's shaking body as she lay there.

The severe flogging she had just endured at the hands of one of the most skilled flogger users in all of Bangkok, if not Thailand, left her body covered in deep red stripes and purple blotches. She had her arms and feet spread-eagle tight, her nipples clamped tight, and her tits pulled away from her body at an impossible length. She had been pushed past her breaking point, and Mary decided it was time to push her over it.

Gently, she pushed the wand up and down, around the clit, pressing it in after each turn. Inga's knees began to shake, she began to sweat profusely and her juice began to drip, her head

began to shake, she began to scream and groan, and finally her head began to shake frantically.

Mary was begged by Inga,

"Plz finger fuck me, plz fuck me with a dildo in my pussy, plz fuck me with whatever you want, plz fuck me now!"

She cried out in pain when Mary stopped using the wand and quickly and violently finger fisted her companion. She continued moving forward because she could feel Inga's climax coming on. She continued to press her fingers in while applying the wand to the throbbing clit with the other hand.

Inga abruptly erupted in a single loud scream, leaping entirely off the bed. She immediately fell back and trembled violently as the aftershocks struck her; it appeared as though an earthquake had hidden downtown San Francisco. Mary released her hand and wand, freed herself from the chains and clamps, and then gently kissed her lover and friend. This was the tale of their friendship, in which they alternatedly gave each other crazed delight.

Mary had everything well planned out; Peyton had finally experienced a true cock fuck, and his lover Inga had experienced a powerful climax. Out of the three women, two expressed satisfaction. When only...

Zeke had been watching the show and massaging his black cock in the background when, as if reading Mary's mind, he approached the girl and pulled her close to him.

CHAPTER 20

She gasped and closed her eyes as he gave her a passionate kiss before grabbing her by the waist, lifting her off the ground, and impaling her on his pulsing cock.

Ezekiel pushed their bodies towards the closest wall, smashed her into it forcefully, and then thrust his cock like a jackhammer into her swollen pussy. They both arrived after only five minutes of good, hard shafting, groaning as they did so. Zeke's manhood was still inside her swollen pussy, which was oozing thick white semen as they dropped to the ground. Now that everything had gone well, Mary was genuinely happy.

The bungalow was virtually empty the following morning because as folks had woken up over the previous evening, they had showered, changed, and left. Arnold in his Chevy pickup, Larry in his Hummer, and Zeke on his Harley. When a cell phone rang, Inga got up to answer it, and as soon as she hung up, she changed, washed, and left with the other females. The girls all ended up sleeping in the enormous bed till daybreak. When she raced out, she left a note for the other two. Mary and Peyton didn't even move.

They didn't get out of bed until mid-morning. They shared a soft, passionate kiss, as lovers frequently do, but Mary rolled out of bed and fled the room before they could get carried away. Ten minutes later, Peyton rose and entered the kitchen where Mary was preparing some freshly squeezed orange juice.

Come on, slackers! Only time for a short juice before we get off on the road; you still have experiences and adventures to have before returning to the United States! Mary placed two juice cups on the counter and said, "We have to dress you in some of me special garments, my friend." She led Peyton to the bedroom and dug around in her closet before throwing out two clothes that appeared to be commonplace but weren't quite right.

The first was an odd bra with cut-outs for the nipples to poke through that was made of black latex. However, that was not all; immediately around the edge of the cut-out there was a ring of thicker latex that housed short, needle-sharp, nearly inflexible nylon pin-pricks. The outfit appeared to be a contemporary adaptation of something made for the Spanish Inquisition.

The second piece of apparel was a pair of high-waisted, high-cut, black latex panties. At first, one may not think these were too strange, but if they were closely examined, they revealed two distinct rubber cocks. The one in the ass region was a shorter — four inch — but much thicker butt plug, also with a thick bulbous head, while the one in the front part of the underwear was an eight-inch-thick dildo complete with moulded veins and a big bulbous head. When worn appropriately, a section of sharp nylon pin pricks that were located on top of the front dildo would rest against the wearer's clit.

Peyton took each thing in turn and simply turned it over and over in her hands, marveling at how it looked and imagined how it would feel to wear it. She wouldn't have to wait long for her

fantasies to come true. She received a nod from Mary directing her to put them on.

She initially put on the bra with Mary's assistance; it was tighter than anything she would often wear and, as soon as she hooked it on, brought tears to her eyes. Mary assisted in centering the nipples in their cut-outs and made sure the cups adequately covered her tits. She then gave them a soft kiss while sucking the nipples to make them stand up straighter, but this only served to press the pin-pricks deeper into the tender flesh. Peyton flinched, and for this she received a slap in the face. She could already feel herself self-creaming.

Mary lubricated the front and back butt plugs of the dildo panty before holding it open while Peyton walked inside and slowly moving it up her legs. When the butt plug made contact with the ass, Mary again helped ease it into the puckered hole, pushed it in an inch, then once again pulled the panties up. First, the dildo touched the pussy and Mary maneuvered it past the already wet labia.

Each inch that the two intruders wormed inside Peyton's flesh evoked a "ooooh!

", "aaaah! ", or "!" she says. When both silicone cocks had finally finished their journey, Mary continued to pull the panties up alongside her until they were fully inserted. Peyton heard a clear click while the panties were being pulled up tight and felt Mary working something behind her back. She then felt her bra being

pulled in slightly and heard another click. When she turned to ask Mary a question, she received yet another slap in return.

She handed Peyton a formal white cotton blouse, which was tight on her and made her bra and erect nipples visible to passersby. "Nothing to worry about my beautiful friend just two little padlocks, I wouldn't want you to remove your pretty underwear if you were to tire of it, I will free you when I see fit, and now for the rest of your wardrobe," she said. Mary then displayed the traditional navy blue business suit she had placed on the bed, complete with a pencil skirt that ended four inches above the knee and a stylish jacket that concealed her bra and nipples. Unless she unbuttoned her jacket, no one would have noticed that she was so demure.

Mary remarked, "Almost finished, my love," as she proceeded to retrieve a pair of blue stilettos with five-inch heels and an odd-looking wide ankle strap. She held the shoes out for Peyton to enter, and when she did, Mary put two tiny padlocks in them and locked them as well. She nearly resembled any Bangkok professional woman at this point.

Peyton hadn't seen the whole picture until Mary led her to a mirror and took her by the arm; Peyton's shock at seeing herself was sufficient evidence of Mary's skill.

Peyton, who had never worn heels higher than two inches, teetered as the two departed the cottage. She was experiencing all kinds of bizarre sensations, such as being hot and cold all over, from the cocks in her ass and pussy.

CHAPTER 21

As soon as she climbed inside, she could feel them being pushed further in. They started driving after she found a more comfortable posture.

They chose a side road into the forest after an hour of highway driving. Peyton noticed a group of buildings off in the distance, and as they approached, she noticed a sign that read, "SNOW STUDIOS, producing images out of your fantasies." Her mouth dropped agape as she realized that these were her late husband's studios. Peyton was still speechless as they exited the vehicle after Mary pulled directly into a marked parking space by the main building. As they walked towards the entrance, Peyton read additional parking signs such as "Mr. G. Snow — Managing Director" and "Ms. E. Klimova — Director(Production)". There were others, but Mary accelerated and she had to give up reading signs.

By this point, Peyton had realized that her husband's business was not a shady one run on a shoestring budget; rather, what she was witnessing was big-budget Hollywood competition, though it would never be able to compete with Hollywood due to the nature of the movies. She also realized that Mary was a significant player here and was immediately beneath her husband in the organization. She should be vigilant about keeping her eyes and ears alert. Just before they entered the two-story building, Mary spoke to her.

"Peyton, today you will discover a little more about the operation your late husband was involved in, my role in it, the other players, and yourself. Now, we'll go to the corporate board meeting. Since you are now the managing director, they are expecting you, which, incidentally, explains the business suit. Following that, we'll go to one of the sound studios where they are filming — you might wind up helping in a movie — before going to the editing room and having supper with the other director, Katerina, also known as Stella.

They entered the reception area, which was made of glass and steel and had a fountain, white leather couches, grey marble floors, and numerous plants. There were erotic-themed sculptures, easels, paintings, and pictures, some of which showed nude models in various stances and others of which showed models engaging in sexual behaviors, some kinky and others not. When the receptionist jumped up and started speaking, Peyton looked about in fascination.

"Miss Watt! " Oh my, we've been waiting for you, Ms. Klimova is upstairs waiting for you with the rest of the board; I'll let them know you're coming, but please let Matika accompany you. Matika appeared out of nowhere, a petite ladyboy with tiny tits and a boyish build. She was dressed in a uniform of a short white skirt, a tight white blouse, and platform wedges, just like the receptionist Cindy, and they both wore name badges. They rode the elevator to the first floor, then followed Matika to the end of the hallway. There, the young Thai knocked on a door marked

"Boardroom." She opened the door and said, "Let the visitors enter," and as she closed it, the young Thai made her way out.

When Mary and Peyton entered the boardroom, a stunningly attractive brunette who appeared to be in her late forties and was seated at the head of the table gave them a curious glance. She grinned at them, and Peyton noticed right once that the smile was hiding venom and loathing—the eyes did not deceive. The lady stood forward and said.

"Mary, welcome back. You must be Peyton, or should I call you Mrs. Snow? We haven't seen you since our previous meeting three months ago. You must be very special to have enticed our Fred to the altar—I had no idea he had wed! 'Join us, there's a lot to talk who had been silent up until this point, took Peyton to the head of the table, turned her to face the board, and then said.

Ladies and gentlemen, I'm Fred Snow's late boss's widow, Mrs. Peyton Garret-Snow. Mrs. Garret-Snow is now the Managing Director of this company, and there is no doubt about it. As such, I would like to lead her to the Chair and be the first to officially welcome her aboard. She then turned to Peyton and said, "Welcome Mrs. Garret-Snow." Peyton grinned and responded, "Thank you."

"Mary, thank you for the warm compliments, but allow me to add a few points. First of all, until my lawyers spoke to me, I was completely unaware of Fred's empire when I first met him. Second, the operation seems to run smoothly, and since I don't fully understand how it works, I'd prefer to leave it in the hands of

the experts. That said, I'm happy to continue serving as managing director and overseeing the entire operation from a distance; I'll only travel to the headquarters for significant board meetings. I shall choose a representative who will hold the same rank as me in my absence to make sure everything runs smoothly; I'll announce their name soon. Thirdly, while you and the board may refer to me as Peyton, I prefer to be addressed professionally as Ms. Snow. The brunette quickly stepped back; Mary grinned and began to explain... "Now I would want to know who everyone here is so if you could be so kind as to introduce everyone," Peyton said, sitting in the chair.

"The board is made up of,"

Director in charge of employees, Ms. Mary Watt, is from Phuket Province in Thailand.

Katerina Klimova, a director in charge of production from Moscow, Russia.

The company's accountant, Mr. Fungus McDermott, is from Glasgow, Scotland (forty years old and slightly effeminate).

Assistant accountant Ms. Kirsty McMonagle, a thirty-year-old blonde from Inverness, Scotland who is also Mr. McDermott's sweetheart.

Chief of Security and native of Cebu City, Philippines, Ms. Beta Duran (short and stocky forty year old bodybuilder, strictly lesbian).

Hawaii-based Ms. Chad Doherty and my assistant (age 22, of Polynesian descent and bi-sexual).

CHAPTER 22

Katerina's assistant, Ms. Maria de Medeiros, is from Lisbon, Portugal (and her 23 year old bi-sexual lover).

Be Knuppe, the Chairman's personal assistant from Rostock, Germany (also believed to be bi-sexual)

Besides, there is one non-voting member,

The Board's Secretary, Ms. Teresa Banham, is a strictly lesbian 21-year-old woman from Richmond, England.

Mary gave a brief introduction to each person, leaving out the details in brackets, which she would later tell to Peyton in private. After being introduced, everyone nodded before getting down to business, reading the minutes, financial report, staff report, security report, any other business, and mundane chit-chat. This went on for three hours, during which Peyton squirmed and sweated in her seat. She was certain that the latex pants were trapping a quart of sweat and juice, and that the bra's pin pricks were causing her nipples to throb. She longed for the meeting to be over and for Mary to free her from these torturous clothing.

As the conference finally concluded and everyone stood up, Katerina approached Mary and completely disregarded what Peyton had to say.

I will provide you a list of impending projects that you will need to immediately endorse. "Mary, I have instructed Ms. Banham to have all the new contracts ready for my approval later this afternoon."

Mary answered,

"Stella, now that Peyton is here, I don't think there is any justification in your signing anything. You have only served as acting chairman while Fred was out of the country and with his written consent; however, now that he is deceased, Peyton is our heir, and it is up to her to decide who represents her when she is not present. Any temporary agreement he may have signed is now void,' Peyton said, placing her hand on Stella's forearm as she spoke softly, causing Stella's eyes to light up and her nostrils to flare.

Peyton said, "I'm going to visit a sound studio first then we can meet for business." This seemed to calm Stella's temper and she nodded assent. Peyton continued, "I'd like to immerse myself in the company some more before I decide who will be my representative while I am away, so I would appreciate it if you wouldn't mind my sitting with you this afternoon as I sign the contracts and you can guide me."

With that, Peyton, Mary, and their helpers Chad and Bella left the conference room. Mary explained to Peyton as they made their way through the studios up until they reached a door labelled "Sound Studio #3," at which point they stopped, he said.

Peyton, we must make sure the light is green before entering; a red light would indicate that the cameras are rolling and we must wait. You, me, Chad, and Fran will be the four of us entering. Then they entered. "The cast and models are eager to greet you."

A long-haired brunette with long hair was bound to a whipping bench in the late 19th century scene being filmed, and a muscular

blonde man was hard-fucking her in the mouth while another man sodomized her. The two heavy weights that were fastened to her stretched nipples caused her tits to hang low. The poor girl was covered with whip marks on her back and behind, and she was crying uncontrollably.

Lights, boom microphones, cables, and cameras—both film and still—were arranged about the bed; the corporation not only produced movies, but also sold magazines and booklets of them. Peyton's nipples were already giving her pain due to having the dildo panties on since breakfast, so the sight of this made her groan. Mary grinned; of course, she knew the secret as Chad and Fran gaped at her.

They spoke with the director and the camera crew as soon as they watched a few takes being recorded before leaving the studio, but not before Peyton had inquired about the identity of the female model and made sure Fran took note of it. There was still time until Peyton's meeting with Stella, so Mary escorted them to the location of Fred's former office. She opened the big oak door that said "Fred Snow — Managing Director" at the corner of the building, and they entered.

Peyton has never been in a more impressive office. It wasn't just an office; it was more like a small apartment with two big TVs, a huge oak desk, Fred's executive chair, and two visitor chairs on the opposite side of the desk. It also had a small boardroom table with six chairs, a big chaise longue, a dining table with six chairs, and two guest chairs.

CHAPTER 23

A fully equipped kitchenette was located in an alcove that Peyton could see. At the end of the room, a sliding partition that was currently only partially open revealed a big king bed, a prie-dieu, and other items that were partially hidden from view.

This workplace is flexible and may, if necessary, serve as someone's home for several weeks. Mary spoke solemnly as he turned to face their assistants.

"Chad, Fran, you both know the regulations of the company, anything you ever see or do behind closed doors is confidential and shall never be disclosed. Breaking this rule results in immediate termination of employment with no references, no severance compensation, and no recourse. You also know that the late Mr. Snow frequently entertained in this office; I have no doubt that you may have participated in such entertainment at one point, but I don't know and I don't care. What matters to me is what happens after this. Peyton is the new owner and MD, but she is also my lover and my sub, and occasionally, we may entertain. If you two would like to be a part of it, please feel free. I can offer you alternate positions in another organization, though, if you want not to be a part of this arrangement. Just let me know right away," Chad said to Fran, who then turned to face Peyton before looking back at her. Deafening quiet prevailed.

Later, they spoke,

Please say yes! Include us! The four women hugged one other tightly and exchanged kisses and smiles. Mary has just made one addition.

"Remember girls, we already know who our biggest enemy is. She is part of us and would destroy the three of us if she could, and now Peyton too. Her ultimate goal is to take over Snow Studios; she thought she had it in her grasp when Fred died, but fortunately I got on the case quickly enough to ensure Peyton remained above suspicion. If we work together, we can defeat her. I want to show that she was responsible for Fred's death. Since Peyton needs to go sign contracts with her in an hour, we must maintain a false sense of security. Fran, you will accompany her; you never leave her with Stella alone, is that clear? She poses a threat.

Fran scowled while concurring. Thank you, my angel; it will be lovely to have you totally on board, Mary remarked as she held her in her arms and kissed her on the lips. She then said, "And now let's make the most of this hour," giving Chad the same response. She led the way into the bedroom and told the other three to strip to their underwear before placing Peyton towards the foot of the bed.

Mary wore merely a pink thong because she didn't need a bra, Chad wore ivory French knickers and a lace bra to support her 38D tits, and Fran donned a lilac pair of cheekini panties and a balconette bra. When they saw what Peyton was wearing, Chad and Fran gasped as they leaned against each other to watch her show off her stunning physique. Peyton patiently waited there.

Mary approached her and carefully unlocked her bra and underwear. After calling the other two over, they showered her with kisses and caresses while slowly taking the two items off. The bra was removed first. Chad unclipped the bra and began to take it off as Fran licked her bruised, purple, and puffy nipples. Mary assisted in removing it completely, and when they did so, they noticed a row of tiny pinholes surrounding her areola, some of which had drawn blood and were painful. Fran better licked them.

They then began to slowly remove the dildo and plug while pulling down her underwear. The plug stopped at the large bulge it had in the center, but the dildo slid out effortlessly. When Fran slowly pulled the plug till it came out with a loud "plop," Chad caressed Peyton's soggy pussy. They played with Peyton by kissing her, stuffing her two hungry holes with their fingers and tongues, giving her love bites on her inner thighs and inner arms, and nibbling on her ears, neck, and thighs. Then they stopped and lay her on the bed, leaving her completely bare while they continued to wear their underwear. It was time for her to enjoy herself, not them.

Mary ate out her pussy using her teeth and tongue on her clit, labia, and hole while Chad and Fran took one tit each and licked, sucked, and nibbled it to the point where Peyton almost jumped off the bed. On few occasions, Peyton screamed, and the Asian had to gag her to quiet her.

They continued the assault for a considerable amount of time until the bed was completely saturated with her juice. Meanwhile, each girl had an impressive wet patch on her crotch, and their underwear were also completely soaked. All four of them were now naked on the bed after ripping off their underpants. After taking off the gag, Chad sat on Peyton's face and wriggled while settling her pussy. Fran was occupied with a gift from Mary, a large black triple strap-on with a large main dildo for the pussy, a thinner one underneath for the asshole, and a short, thick dildo for the wearer on the inside of the harness. Fran pushed in the wearer's rubber cock, then tightened the harness around her waist and climbed to the edge of the bed.

She shoved the anal dildo into Peyton's still-gaping hole after nudging Peyton's wet pussy with it. Peyton gasped as Fran inserted it completely before beginning to slowly move it in and out. At the same time, Chad was being devoured by Peyton, who was savoring her freshly-shaved, coconut-flavored pussy. Fran and Chad fondled one other's tits as they leaned in close to each other and began kissing.

Mary, meantime, proceeded around the bed with two lubricated huge Princess Plugs, inserting one in Fran and then another in Chad. The girls protested, but Mary simply quelled them. As their asses felt full, they increased their efforts. Fran fucked Peyton harder as Chad used all of her strength to crush her face against the ground.

CHAPTER 24

Peyton was overjoyed since she had been primed all morning in her underpants, the dildos front and back had stretched her, and the punishment bar's pin pricks had nearly driven her nuts because they kept piercing her areola. Nearly since the minute they left Mary's home, she had been drenched.

Mary then retrieved three pairs of nipples clamps. With rubber teeth and screw adjustability, they're not too severe. Each girl squealed when her nipples were clamped, but none of them objected when she clipped them on all the exposed nipples. She then connected Chad's and Fran's tits such that any movement made by one of them would stretch the tits of the other. She then took the long flogger, which had a ten inch cock-shaped handle and at least one hundred thin leather strands that were each twenty inches long. She also hooked Peytons, one to Fran and one to Chad.

Mary began to flogger the girls on the bed as she walked about them at random, sometimes hitting Chad's back, Fran's ass, Peyton's thighs, or any other tit, or even their feet, legs, or arms. The girls never knew where she would strike next as her strokes began increasing stronger and more frequent. While Peyton was driving her tongue to inconceivable depths in Chad's pussy, Fran was piercing Peyton as hard as she could.

Mary stopped moving and stood behind Fran. Focusing on Fran's buttocks, she encouraged her with the flogger. Her strokes were quick and fierce, and they were followed by shouts from her

victim. Fran fucked Peyton as if there was no tomorrow as a result. Peyton must have sensed this as well because she intensified her efforts to savor Chad's delicious pussy, which had been drenching her face for some time by this point. Fran felt an almost imperceptible heat rising from her innermost soul and a tremble, almost a quake as her orgasm crept in.

Chad appeared to be focused and deep in thought as she gritted her teeth and had her eyes closed. All of a sudden, she let out a 'oooohhh!

Along with a "aaaahhh!

'. A roar that seemed to emanate from her own interior caused her to grit her teeth and open her mouth widely. As climax after climax tore through her body, she trembled like a leaf and let forth a banshee shriek.

This had the desired effect on Peyton, who appeared to shudder on the bed and tremble and leap as if she were possessed when her orgasm hit her. Although she was unable to scream since Chad's pussy was still on her face, a keening sound did come from between her legs. Being a squirter, she came in full power and pumped pussy cum all over Fran's legs.

Fran, poor Fran, was the first to experience the orgasm approach as a heat built up inside of her, but she had not yet succeeded. Nevertheless, when Peyton's hot pussy juice struck her pussy and legs, this did it for her, and she came with an enormous yell, pumping away like a madman. The three collapsed into a heap,

and Mary was pleased since it would strengthen their teamwork and relationship.

The girls all made their way to the shower area that was next to the bedroom. There was a large wet floor shower that could fit at least eight people, with a marble bench along one wall and a glass wall on the other. The shower had a variety of shower heads dispersed throughout, as well as rings set in various locations in the marble wall and bars sporadically throughout. just not right now.

All the girls now required was a leisurely shower to remove the dirt and sweat they had accumulated. They played around for a while lathering each other. Following their showers, they all changed into soft towels with the monogram "Snow Studios" and made their way to the main office where Mary had already laid out sandwiches, snacks, and drinks that had been purchased from the catering department.

They ate and chatted nonstop till the dishes were empty since they were ravenous and attacked the meal with zeal. Mary then spoke. Ladies, pay close attention; there are contracts to be signed. Ekaterina (also known as Stella) planned to sign them alone, as she normally did when Fred was gone, but Peyton threw a wrench in the plan by imposing her authority as Fred's owner and legal heir. This means that Peyton, who was astute enough to ask Stella for guidance, will now sign the contracts. Of course, to further put Stella in her place, Peyton will not accompany Stella to her office; instead, she will send for her and inform her that the documents

will be signed there. It ought to seriously bruise her ego. Fran, you will stay with them at all costs and you can count on Maria to be with Stella. If you need assistance, call Fungus or Kirsty; they are unquestionably on our side. We have some excavating to do and won't be back until after supper, so I must go with Chad. Best of luck.

When they emerged, Mary informed Peyton that she had taken the initiative the day before to order the restocking of the bedroom walk-in closet with a variety of clothes, underwear, and shoes for Peyton to wear whenever she was in town and stopped by the studios. Mary also added that she had already laid out what Peyton needed to wear for the meeting with Stella.

Once they had departed, Peyton went into the bedroom and discovered a pair of black 4-inch court shoes, an ivory embroidered cotton blouse, a light grey miniskirt, and a set of lilac lace balconette bra and thong under the covers. Peyton considered that it wasn't too raunchy or too subdued. Peyton sat at the boardroom table to wait as Fran informed her that she had emailed Stella, who was apparently not too happy about having to come to Peyton's office based on the curt reply. Fran was already dressed in her professional attire when Peyton returned to the main office. They didn't have long to wait; ten minutes later there was a knock on the door, and Peyton requested Fran to open it as Stella and Maria stood there fumbling with a pile of documents. While Fran sat across from her, Peyton remained seated and invited Stella and Maria to join her at the table.

CHAPTER 25

She seated them on either side of her. The contracts were laid out on the table after the formalities and platitudes, and things got down to business.

Without a question, Stella was excellent at her work; she knew who to sign up with and under what conditions, she briefed Peyton well, and they breezed through the majority of the contracts. Even though Maria's English wasn't always perfect, she was effective and good. As they were down to the final five, Peyton noticed that not everything was completely obvious. The numbers didn't make sense to her, and she asked questions that, even if Stella was providing appropriate answers, appeared to make Maria anxious, as evidenced by her excessive squirming and lip-biting.

Peyton realized Fran had noticed as well, and when Stella recommended they take a break for tea, Peyton wondered whether they would need to call for assistance. Maria offered to prepare the tea and walked to the kitchenette after Peyton agreed that she might have some time to contemplate. In a short while, she returned with a pot of tea and four cups, which she distributed before they started sipping and engaging in some light conversation.

When Stella would lean over to speak to her "in confidence," Peyton would feel Stella's breasts on her arm and the Russian's nipples stiff against her upper arm, which both made her uneasy and excited. Peyton also observed that Stella kept brushing her hand and placing her hand on her knee.

After some time, Peyton experienced lightheadedness. She assumed it was caused by fatigue and strain from wearing the dildo panties for such a prolonged period of time. She began to sweat profusely and felt her limbs sag; she also had a pressing need to use the restroom. Fran got up to assist her and proceeded towards her before collapsing in a heap when she stood up and took a stride while tripping. Peyton attempted to scream, but her voice only made a whisper. She then saw Maria — or was it two Marias? — reach out to her. Before there was silence, the room appeared to be spinning faster and faster.

The contracts, the tea, and even the scent of Stella's perfume were all gone when Fran awoke. There was not even the slightest hint that they had ever been here. She made an effort to maintain her composure. First, she looked at her phone; the email she had written to Stella and its response were both gone. Next, she looked at the office security camera; static; that was all that was visible, and the machine was giving an error message. Really bad.

When the phone rang, she had just sent Mary a quick message and was composing an email for her.

'Fran! What on earth just happened? Chad and I discovered enough evidence to conclude that Stella might have been involved in Fred's killing, and I was ready to look into this further when your message arrived. Peyton is in severe danger as a result. We are aware that Stella intends to take over the business, but because Peyton has assumed her proper position, the only way she can do so is if she can convince Peyton to turn the firm over to her. Fran

began to sob as the reality of what had happened hit her; Peyton had been abducted and there was no proof the abductors had even been present; only her, and she was afraid of being held responsible. Fran, go meet Fungus and Kirsty and work with them; Chad and I still need to be here for a while, said Mary. Oh, and if his secretary tries to delay you, just let her know that you want him to find a malt for you.' Fran hung up the phone without even bothering to ask what was going on.

After locking up the office, she ran to the finance department where she approached Fungus' secretary, Fiona Samuel, and informed her that she needed to see Fungus immediately. Fiona began to explain that Mr. McDermott was scheduled for a meeting and would not be available today. She continued by saying that perhaps next week he might have a free slot, but Fran cut her off. Fiona paused, stood up, and said to Fran, "Fran, follow me." She then went through a door, down a short corridor, and ultimately through a padded soundproof door. "Fiona, I need Mr. McDermott to get a malt for me." She was greeted by a spectacle that would go down in history. Mr. McDermott, Fungus, was lying on the ground in the doggy position, sporting a leather harness, a butt plug poking out of his ass, and weights dangling from clamps that were tightly secured to his nipples. He was giving a blow-job to a very young model who continued ramming his enormous cock into Fungus's mouth while Kirsty, his assistant, was also giving him a blow-job while she fucked him with a gigantic strap-on.

They instantly stopped when Fiona and Fran entered.

She spoke as Kirsty and Fungus swiftly rose to their feet.
"Fiona, we are aware that you would only interrupt us in an emergency, and if Fran is with you, then we are aware that Peyton is the subject of the emergency. Fran, Mary has been keeping us informed of current developments and has warned us that something might happen, which is why we established the code word "malt." After dismissing the model and taking off everything he was wearing, Fungus said, "I'll be with you as soon as we get dressed. " Fungus then changed into a chambray shirt and chinos. They left the room and entered their sizable conference room after Kirsty removed her harness and put on a white cotton g-string and a floral summer dress.
While Fran was telling her narrative, the other three were seated at the table and kept questioning her who said what and when, who moved where, and what she did. This took little more than 30 minutes, yet by the end Fungus, Kirsty, and Fiona knew just as much as if they had been present.
Kirsty said.
"I believe it is safe to assume that Stella and Maria would have relocated Peyton away from the studios. They will need a private location and time for Peyton to execute a power of attorney or power of representation in their favor. We must find Peyton during this time because if Stella takes over the business, we will be lost. If Peyton is as strong as I believe her to be based on what I saw this morning, she will be able to hold out for some time.
Where, though, could she have hid her?

CHAPTER 26

Fran enquired as she peered around. The other girls were giving Fungus anxious looks as well, but they all observed that he was sporting a smug expression. They gave him puzzled looks.

Ladies, I think I might finally have the upper hand.

I handle all of the company's transactions, and the rules indicate that any transaction involving a board member that is worth more than $100,000 must go through me, he stammered as he always did when he was anxious. W-w-well... When Ms. Klimova bought an abandoned fort near Phra Pradaeng, she initially claimed it was for location filming before revealing that it was for her personal use as a corporate retreat. Once she purchased it, nothing more was heard; let's have a look there.

Kirsty approached Fungus and gave him a lips kiss.

You are a rock star, Fungus! Get out more about this fort's location so we can go find it. When her phone was out of service when she tried to call Mary, she left her a message and they came up with a plan. Fran and Kirsty would ask Beta to organize a security detail and two 4x4s because, if their suspicions were true, they would need some muscle. Fungus and Fiona would investigate the records to identify the property deeds of the fort and obtain its coordinates.

Beta was discovered in her tiny office in the basement, where she was as usual sitting in the observation booth and viewing security footage and reports. Beta glanced up somewhat astonished when Kirsty rapped on the glass enclosing the booth because she wasn't

used to having other board members visit her. She left the booth and moved with her visitors to her desk before standing up but not before calling in a replacement to continue checking the screens. When Beta grew more concerned and spoke in her peculiar mashup of American English and Spanish, Fran and Kirsty described the problem to her.

"Yes, ma'am! Peyton, the seorita, has been abducted by katerina, the puta who just wants the business for herself. You stay calm my nia, Beta will make sure we succeed," she said, picking up the phone and starting to speak in a rapid-fire mix of Spanish, Filipino, and English with a few sprinklings of English. "I will put together a good team, not just any team, but el mejor," she added. "You two need to change into more appropriate attire, anything you can get dirty in, and go meet me in the garage in 30 minutes, vengeance!" '

They proceeded to their respective offices to change because Fran was still wearing her formal working attire and Kirsty was wearing a thin summer dress. Board members and other senior staff members also had small bedrooms they could use for overnight visits, and every Snow Studios employee had at least one wardrobe in the studios where they kept their numerous costumes.

The girls chose white T-shirts, cargo pants, beige in both cases, and work boots over plain, comfy underwear because they had decided to dress in a rough manner. They then called Fiona and Fungus to inform them of the plans before continuing. Fran was

picked up from her workplace by Kirsty, who arrived first, and the two of them rode the elevator down to the garage. As they arrived, they discovered Fungus and Fiona waiting for them. Fiona was dressed in beige cargo trousers and a red T-shirt, while Fungus was wearing pink and camouflage cargo pants.

They didn't have long to wait since two enormous black Humvees halted as they emerged from the garage's underground levels. Beta got out of the first vehicle while the security detail got out of the second. Afterwards Beta introduced the detail members.

"Ladies and gentlemen, I present my "B" team. You might wonder why not the "A" team. They are the "Best" squad since mine are the Best and theirs is a TV joke. I would trust Amelia, Bea, Gloria, and Dara with my life. They are all skilled with all weaponry and skilled in hand-to-hand combat. Moreover, Dara is a skilled driver and will operate vehicle 2. Bea is an expert in explosives, Gloria is a communications and surveillance pro, and Amelia is a master archer. You four will ride in vehicle 1, which I will drive; Mr. McDermott, do you have the necessary coordinates? '

Beta entered the GPS coordinates that Fungus had given her into the Humvee's navigation system and let the computer figure out the best course of action. She continued,

Team, I want to do it in one and a half hours, but the navigation computer estimates that it will take us two hours.

Once the security team arrived in vehicle 2, the four companions jumped into Beta's car. After quickly leaving the garage and heading out into the open road.

The following hour was hell for them as all kinds of scenarios ran through their heads. The four of them saw Peyton being tortured into signing or being forced to sign under threat of death. They also imagined Peyton being fatally wounded and being left to die. Finally, they imagined Peyton being drugged to sign. The earlier they arrived, the better.

Beta had contacted Mary along the way to update her on the situation and to discuss her plans. Mary informed Beta that she would explain later, but for the time being they were on their own because she was unable to contact the police due to specific information she had just discovered in the previous two hours.

They made a detour onto a side road that led directly into the Bangkok jungle, a mountainous area of woods that appeared eerie in the waning light. The SatNav kept them on this road for almost twenty minutes before switching to a bumpy, pothole-filled dirt road, but the Humvee handled this with ease.

They slowed down when they spotted the shadowy form of tall walls in the distance, and Beta shut off the truck's lights. They stopped the two vehicles after gently approaching the edge of the wooded cover, then they got out in silence. Beta addressed her crew first, then the four company members, using her throat mike.

"This is the property; we will approach gently and make sure they are present before proceeding." You will now follow my directions, do you understand? Fungus nodded in agreement and complied with Beta.

CHAPTER 27

They could see a lit building through the fort's walls, where loud noises and yells could be heard occasionally, along with what appeared to be periodic screams, up ahead. Beta instructed her squad to conduct a reconnaissance and report back. The girls vanished into the shadows like wraiths, and nothing seemed to be happening until Beta's radio began to crackle and she spoke to Fungus and the others in Filipino.

"Ms. McMonagle, Mrs. Knuppe, Mr. McDermott, and Ms. Samuel, the situation is dire; we must enter immediately." You four must remain here despite its appearance, Beta said as she pulled her sidearm and vanished into the shadows.

She was restrained, her hands bound to the bench. pulling down her underwear... Sister Anne, the housekeeper, spoke in a booming voice. the sensation of leather against her ass, the relentless, merciless blows... the sound of a strap on exposed skin, a teenager being beaten, or sounds of a struggle...

'Noooo! Kindly, Sister! Please trust me when I say that I didn't do anything. I never took the rosary, and I have no idea how it ended up on my nightstand. Sister Anne, if you would kindly believe me! Stop! Please stop, it hurts too much! '

She sobbed uncontrollably for a while as the strap pounded repeatedly on her naked behind, but Sister Ann never even responded.

'Thief! Thief! Thief! '...

...'Thief! Thief! Thief! You took my business! Fred was merely my cameraman, but he eventually became the owner of the entire business since he helped me out when I needed a loan, and now that you had to show up, I almost had it back! Thief! You will sign authority over to me once I beat you senseless! The business should be mine by right! '

Peyton's consciousness was in and out of focus. Was the agony from the strap squeezing her ass actually there? Where did she go? Who were these women, who she could barely make out in haze? Brother Anne? Mary the sister? were they? Why weren't they dressed in their wimples or habits?

Sister, please! The rosary wasn't taken from me! Mercy, Sister Ann, please! She sobbed uncontrollably, yet the words of the Sister kept ringing in her ears.

'Thief! You took what belonged to me! Thief! '...

...'Thief! To take over my business, you wed Fred! He must have informed you that he was the owner of a movie studio! Stella continued to yell at Peyton as she brutally beat her. The poor girl's ass was covered in bruises, and there were small beads of blood forming where the strap's tip had struck her.

Stella's arm was briefly grasped by the Portuguese aide Maria as she spoke.

'Senhora Ekaterina, take a rest right now; let the little girl recover for a few minutes if not, she will be useless to us.

Stella's eyes were on fire as she regarded her, but the flame quickly subsided.

Maria said, "You are correct, we need to give Peyton some time to recuperate. She is delirious, and the drug you gave her combined with the beating is causing her to have hallucinations." Maria then turned to face Peyton's bare body and licked her lips. "Ela needs to have her bun and bottom badly bitten, Sentress!" Please allow me to do it with a strap, Senhora? Stella responded, "My little one, later," I said. But first, we need her to sign the power of attorney so you can receive your reward. After you've had your fill of her, our American friend would benefit from a minor car accident.

Once more, Peyton was unconscious; they gave her some time to recover before shaking her awake. Stella talked with her,

Peyton, pay close attention—do you recognize me? Can you plainly see me? I, who? Peyton gave her a nod and stared at her, she said.

Stella to her pals, is Ekaterina Klimova. Why have you been beating me, why am I tied down, and where am I? She was now fully awake and attentive; there was no longer any fuzziness. Stella talked with her,

Peyton, it doesn't matter where we are; all that counts is that your friends won't ever be able to locate you, or at the very least, not alive. I must first tell you a story before I can respond to your other queries...]

Ten years ago, I was the only proprietor of a tiny pornographic film business called "Ova Pictures," which was profitable. Fred, a promising young cameraman, was then hired, and the revenue

tripled. He wasn't just terrific; he was outstanding, making any scene memorable. He made almost as much money as I did as a cameraman! But I made a mistake and neglected to give the neighborhood gang their protection money. The next month, the police conducted a raid on the studios, discovered drugs and copies of snuff movies in my office, shut down the business, and imprisoned me. Fred was fortunate in that he was not officially listed and was therefore never arrested. To remove the evidence, I had to buy off the mob and the corrupt police head for half a million US dollars. On the condition that I hand the business over to him, Fred was willing to put up the cash. In exchange, he promised that I would serve as his backup and take over if he ever quit or vanished. I consented, we signed the agreement, the evidence vanished, and I was freed. Together, Fred and I transformed the studios when he reopened them under the new name. You see, my lovely Peyton, I have a claim to the business!

Peyton responded in a split second,

"Stella, I have no reason to doubt your account, but I would rather that we return to the studios and have a board-wide discussion about it there. Why did Fred appoint two Directors equally if he wanted you to succeed him? Sorry, I won't sign anything just yet.

Stella's face grew furious, and she yelled at Peyton and told her to get the knout before turning to Maria.

"Oh, well, does the new chick want to play tough?" Since Ivan the Great devised the Russian knout—twenty rawhide strips, each two feet long with a knot every three inches—it has been used to break

tens of thousands of opponents of the regime. I will use it to break you! Remember that it has also claimed hundreds of lives! She then walked back a little distance after grabbing Maria's knout.

Peyton didn't scream for five full seconds after the blow was delivered to her buttocks; instead, the victim let out a loud thud. She then raised the object again, this time aiming lower down the buttocks, which caused the victim to scream once again. Peyton screamed like a banshee as the following blow landed just on the bottom border of the buttocks.

When some of the rawhide knots had drawn blood, Stella paused and straightened them out. She then cleansed the area with a wet chamois. She asked Peyton if she was prepared to sign a contract while she was still crying and grinned at her.

'No! never ever! yelled Peyton in between tears. Few people are aware that the intersection of the thigh and buttocks is one of the body's most sensitive areas, so Stella elevated her knout once more, landing the following stroke there. When another and then another stroke struck her in the same place, Peyton yelled in agony and did not have time to recover. then came a halt.

Ready to sign?" Because if the response is "No" once more, I'll pick up my knuckles this time and won't let up until I've killed or broken you. In either scenario, the business is now mine! When Maria clutched her arm and said once more, she raised her knout, "Minha Senhora, killing her will result in explanations to the police.

CHAPTER 29

" Maria's intervention infuriated Stella, who swung her knout violently at her while not paying attention to where she was striking. "Let me try again," she said. Maria knelt to the ground and screamed in fear as Stella tore the tiny dress off Maria to give her a better punch. Maria covered her head with her arms. On Maria's back and buttocks, fresh wounds were visible; some were dark purple, while others had streaks of caked blood.

Not only that, but Maria's back also displayed old scars that were a result of years of torture at the hands of a stronger person than herself. Maria was knocked over by Stella, who yelled at her to leave the space since she didn't need Maria's assistance to shatter Peyton. When Maria hurried out of the room, she glanced back to the American.

Back to Peyton, Stella raised her arm once more, preparing to let the knout fall once more.

Beta moved through the darkness like a shadow, joining the rest of her crew in a matter of seconds as they all put on night vision rebreather masks. The crew deployed after Beta raised her hand and made a couple hand signs. Gloria and she prepared to smash down the entry door while Amelia sought cover behind a tree blocking the entrance, Bea and Dara took a window to the left of the entrance door, and they established positions. As Stella yelled at Maria, they watched from where they were standing and heard the sounds of leather rubbing against flesh.

Beta gestured with her hand, Bea tossed a smoke grenade through the open window, and Beta and Gloria used a ram to smash in the door at the same time. Beta and Gloria rush in the door as Bea and Dara climb in via the window. There were yells and screams, muted explosions, and smoke coming from the structure.

Amelia pulled her bow and shot an arrow with a tranquilizer head at the person she saw jumping out of a window farther away and trying to flee. The person fell almost instantly. In five minutes, all was finished. Gloria and Dara carried Peyton as Gloria and Beta dragged a handcuffed Stella. Maria was Amelia's target, so she flung her over her shoulder and followed the others back.

When they arrived back at the Humvees, they paused to wait for Bea because her duty wasn't finished yet. At this point, the four board members ran up to help lift Peyton but Beta shooed them away. While they waited, they gently placed Peyton face down in the back of the other Humvee after giving her a sedative shot, while they secured Stella and Maria in the back of the other.

They all climbed inside and waited. After a short while, Bea emerged running quickly. She jumped into the second Humvee, and the two vehicles took off at a high speed. A fireball appeared behind them and an explosion was heard thirty seconds later; the fort building had been destroyed, providing Stella and her mob allies with no more cover.

They moved more slowly on the way back to the studios than they had on the way there because they didn't want to take a chance on getting pulled over by the police and having to defend the two

handcuffed women. Beta contacted Mary while they were traveling and told her they had succeeded; she smiled as she told her this and simply nodded in response to what Mary said.

Since they had called ahead, a stretcher was waiting for Peyton when they arrived back at the studios, which was almost three in the morning. She was carefully placed on it by the waiting medics, who then hurried her to the hospital wing so that the resident medical staff, led by Dr. Marguerite Sablière, could see to her. Before they could start her recovery, they had to examine her and determine the extent of the injuries she had sustained.

Before Fran and the others could congratulate Beta and her team, they vanished into the background. Fran made a mental point to tell Mary what a great job they had done. The four of them decided to go out for a nightcap after talking for a while and realizing they were still too enthusiastic to go to sleep. Kirsty requested that they accompany her to her apartment in the accommodations wing. She had never bothered looking for a place to live in Bangkok because she was satisfied with the temporary apartment she had been given.

They all sat down on the sofas and settee in her spacious living room as she opened the door. There was a wet bar in the corner, and she urged everyone to help themselves. Once everyone had their first drink, they relaxed and chatted for a while before having their second and third.

When she danced in front of the others while still wearing only her simple white cotton underpants, Kirsty got up, turned on some

music, and caressed her body to the beat. With the exception of her basic pink pants, Fiona joined her on the carpet after taking everything off. Also, they tenderly and sensually touched and kissed one another while allowing their hands wander over one another's body.

Fran, who felt left out, made the decision to join in. She undressed but kept her simple blue thong on and joined the other two girls. They danced and caressed until it became too difficult for them to remain upright. They then laid down on the enormous wool rug, abandoning their underwear in the process, and very quickly they were all over one another. They appeared to be one undulating monster with six arms and six legs.

As Fungus slowly rubbed his cock over his boxers while watching the scene, he removed his T-shirt and slacks. The females had formed an intriguing grouping by this point. Fran was sprawled out on the ground while Kirsty licked her nipples and sucked her tits and Fiona devoured her pussy, giving her the licking of her life. Fiona used her fingers to push in two then three digits up to the knuckles, making sure they were well coated in pussy fluid before she slowly slipped her middle finger in Fran's asshole. Fran moaned and fidgeted and was getting extremely wet.

Fran arched her back off the mat as a result, but Kirsty pushed her back down again. She then stopped and gave Fran a heartfelt, lengthy, passionate kiss in the mouth. Fran said in return, "I love this." While doing this, Fiona simultaneously finger fisted her in her pussy and ass, gradually raising her temperature.

CHAPTER 30

Fungus approached the girls when Kirsty called him over and he took off his underwear. She twisted the girl's head and told him to fuck Fran in the mouth. She held his balls and gently squeezed them as he slowly inserted his large circumcised cock into Fran's expectant mouth. Fungus glanced at Kirsty and mouthed the word "please" after she had sucked him for a time, making his cock quiver and turn a deep crimson. Kirsty was aware of his needs and gave it to him.

While Fungus was bisexual, his preference for young males predominated. He was also incredibly submissive, and Kirsty was his Domme. He would fuck anything if Kirsty required it of him. Kirsty had also taught him how to please a woman, and he had mastered the art with the aid of the cane and the tawse. He adored his tiny toys, though, and frequently pleaded with Kirsty to allow him use them during their sex-play.

She stood up and removed a few items from a cabinet drawer before returning and firmly inserting an extra-large Princess Plug into Fungus's asshole. While she did this, he moaned and took his cock out of Fran's mouth to give it to Kirsty. She grabbed a small leather strap, wrapped it over his cock and balls, and buckled it firmly. Next, she grabbed a second, wider strap, and buckled it slightly above his balls. She then took a cum stopper, greased it thoroughly, and forced it forcefully into his pee hole until the cock ring slipped beyond the glans and snuggled under it. This drew his balls away from his cock, which was now thick and purple.

As Fungus shuffled forward, Kirsty moved Fiona out of the way and angled Fran's legs. His big glans prodded her pussy, and Kirsty grabbed it and inserted it into Fran's receptive hole. She then prodded Fungus farther forward until his cock fully filled her wet hole. As he penetrated her, she felt his thickness and how it throbbed, the cock ring pushing against her clit.

Fiona, who was determined that she would not be left out of this, lowered herself to a knee and knelt on Fran's face before adjusting her nipples and speaking angrily.

"Eat me out, lady!" You must take me out to dine! She was so hot already from everything that she was begging for an orgasm. Fungus would behave well knowing that if he let Kirsty down, he would be very sorry for the next few days, if not weeks. Kirsty grinned at this and then left Fungus to screw Fran unattended.

As Fran was eating her out, Kirsty went to get a magic wand and plugged it in before playing it on Fiona's clit. Fiona yelped as she first felt the vibrations on her little button and found it difficult to stay on Fran's face with all that. She wanted to writhe more and more as Kirsty used it on her.

Fran was the first to experience the gradual onset of a group orgasm. Fungus's onslaught of his enormous cock was simply too much for her to handle, and she struggled to raise herself up off the floor as wave after wave of orgasmic bliss struck her. She bit down on Fiona's clit during her peak, sending both of them over the edge and eliciting cries and shouts in response. Two contented females.

With his cock and ball restraints on, Fungus was unable to cum, so Kirsty grinned and pulled back on him. She then pushed him back onto the mat and straddled him, riding him for about five minutes before cumming. She returned to the rug, content, as Fungus regarded her with beseeching eyes.

No, Fungus, not this time. Your time will come. You aren't allowed a climax just yet.

Sister Florence, please. I need some water. I'm so thirsty. Peyton screamed like a baby as the anguish tore through her, eventually sobbing herself to sleep. "Sister, my backside hurts so much, my thighs, please, I need more lotion," she pleaded. In the pitch black, she awoke... Sister Florence, are you there? Why did Sister Agnes have to beat me so severely, Sister? I swear I didn't take her rosary! The young girl began to cry and begged her sister to "tell her please." After a time, she stopped.

'...Sisterrrr!!! Please give me more lotion, Mommy, it hurts so bad! Who is my mother? Florence, Sister! Do I still have Sister Agnes' ire? Please don't let her get near me; she caused me a lot of pain. I need my mother! '

'...Nurse... I need some water. I'm so thirsty. Peyton cried like a baby as the anguish tore through her; eventually, she sobbed herself to sleep. "Nurse, my behind aches so much, my thighs, please, I need more lotion," she pleaded. In the pitch black, she awoke... Are you there, nurse? After crying for a bit, Peyton stopped crying.

CHAPTER 31

With a start, Peyton opened her eyes. She was face down and experiencing excruciating rear numbness; there was no longer any agony. What time was it, the sun was shining through the windows? That was what day of the week? Peyton was in excruciating pain as she struggled to move and cried out in her full confusion.

The cry summoned the nurses, who entered hastily behind a stunningly attractive woman wearing a white lab coat. She turned to face Peyton and grinned warmly. Peyton felt more at comfortable after this, and he questioned them:

"Wound up where? What took place? I'm missing my friends. The other people in the room started to laugh, so the woman in the white lab coat approached her and dragged a stool over to the bed where she sat and responded,

'Madame Snow, you were brought in three days ago and are currently in the studio's medical wing. Staff Nurse Jones will respond to your inquiries on behalf of myself, Dr. Marguerite Sablière. Peyton attempted to get up but realized she was bound to the bed and quite naked. "Now you need your rest. I will let your friends know you are awake and they can see you later." Staff Nurse Jones approached her and muttered, "Please, I need everything explained.

"Ms. Snow, get some rest." Your legs, buttocks, and back were severely injured when you were brought in; this injury was likely caused by some sort of whip, and it took a lot of effort to ensure

that your spine wasn't permanently altered. Although Dr. Sablière has worked extremely hard on you, certain markings are regrettably permanent; the offender should serve a lengthy prison sentence! Peyton shook her head in agreement before closing her eyes and laying her head down to slumber.

The next time she awoke, it was in the late afternoon. Two nurses arrived after she touched the call button, and one of them talked.

"Ms. Snow, the doctor has instructed us to apply some of this aloe gel on your scars before turning you over so that you can begin your recovery process." Peyton found that hearing "We've brought you a nightdress, you have visitors later" made her feel better because she was itching to chat to others and return to normal life. The nurses helped her get up and put on a pink nightgown that looked like a T-shirt with three buttons down the front and little flowers embroidered on it. This made Peyton cry as she recalled the nightmares she experienced the first two nights on the medical wing; it was extremely feminine. She jumped when she heard a tap on the door because she thought Sister Agnes would enter carrying her large strap.

It appeared as though a large delegation had entered! They were all gathered around the bed, staring at her, including Mary, Chad, Fran, Fungus, Kirsty, and a young girl with curly hair she didn't recognize. Mary spoke.

Peyton, we have worried about you nonstop for the past three days, but the doctor has assured us that you are now making

progress toward recovery. After you leave the hospital wing in a few days, your options will be open to you.

Peyton was really curious and wanted to know what had happened to Stella and Maria. What happened to her late husband's body after it was cremated? Who was her rescuer? Who was the adorable girl with the curly hair who kept grinning and had a sparkle in her eyes at her? One by one, each of their inquiries was addressed as the answers flowed thick and fast.

Mary took the lead.

"So, Chad and I went to Stella's flat in downtown Bangkok first, broke in, searched the property, and discovered evidence that Stella had ties to organized crime and was in fact producing snuff films at the time she was incarcerated all those years ago. As we followed up on the names and numbers in the notebook, we discovered that every time she performed for Fred, she had been siphoning money into a covert private account. Also, we discovered she had a second home in the woods; when we got there, we discovered Fred's missing clothes in addition to enough pills to kill the entire board of directors.

Chad went on,

"Mary alerted her colleagues at police headquarters, and they dispatched a forensics team over there. As soon as we heard that you had captured Stella and Maria, we hurried over here to speak with them," the team member said. We asked them questions independently and used the good-cop/bad-cop scenario. Even when confronted with the facts we had obtained, Stella initially

made no admissions. Maria eventually gave in because Mary had threatened to ensure that she would spend at least thirty years in the most difficult prison for women in Thailand, where the suicide rate was the highest, and that if she survived, they would deport her and seize any money she had in any financial institution.

'Maria negotiated a deal and admitted to everything, but of course insisted she was simply doing Stella's bidding,' continued Mary. 'Then we went to Stella and recounted what Maria had said, and Stella tried to cut a deal, but it was too late; Maria had arrived first. Stella is likely to receive a sentence of thirty to life in prison, while Maria, who was following orders and struck a bargain, is likely to be released after eight to ten. The police found enough evidence to charge them both with murder.

Fran now spoke,

The entire board was present for your husband's cremation yesterday; the ashes are currently in an urn in your office; you decide what you will do with them.

Next, Fungus spoke.

The rest of us here organized the rescue, but Beta and four of her girls—Amelia, Bea, Gloria, and Dara—expertly carried it out with the exception of Mary and Chad, who were looking into Stella. It was thrilling but risky.

When Kirsty finally spoke,

"Peyton, this adorable young lady with the sparkling eyes is Fiona. She works as the accounting section's secretary and receptionist and has put in a ton of effort since the day she started here."

CHAPTER 32

Peyton then spoke after turning to face Fiona and the others.

"I am very appreciative of everything you have done for me; you have no idea how much it means to me. I'm hopeful that my memory will eventually return because I still have gaps in it, particularly between being in my workplace and waking up here.

Staff Nurse Jones entered and shooed everyone out since Peyton wanted to rest. "As soon as I am out of here, we need to call an urgent board meeting to nominate two new people to the vacant posts." She gave her a medication as soon as they were outside, and she fell asleep.

body. She also noticed that the bed and her legs were both wet, but it wasn't urine! She reached her initial climax.

As Peyton woke up in the hospital, she was aware of her surroundings, her identity, and the fact that she had just experienced a climax, which had caused her to pee the bed. But, who?

Fungus was completely naked and had twelve purple welts on his ass from a caning he had just got from Kirsty as he stood in one corner of her living room with his nose to the wall and his hands on his head. His face was smeared with the tears he had shed, and he continued to whimper. They were absolutely parallel and spaced from the center of the buttocks to the thighs. One stockinged leg was crossed over the other as Kirsty sat on a sofa wearing slingbacks with her shoe hanging from her foot. She turned to face him and said,

"You are disgusting!" You have no right to inform Peyton that the rescue was "exciting but risky," as the woman is already healing from a traumatic experience and doesn't need to be concerned about us. You heartless jerk! You haven't been permitted to climax for a full month; tonight, I was going to blow you off and let you cum as a treat for acting so well during the rescue, but now you have to anticipate an evening of suffering! I'm debating locking your cock in your tiny cage and denying you climax for at least another month. Don't dare go till I say to, and stay put! I'll definitely be having an orgasm tonight, but you won't! The doorbell rang, so Kirsty got up and went outside to answer it.

With a short, black dress that only reached her mid-thigh, Fiona stood there with her hands in the air. She had bare feet and was walking in black stiletto sandals. Kirsty gave her a smile as she turned to face her and followed her gaze down to her toes. White slingback shoes, ivory self-supporting stockings, and a white minidress were all that Kirsty was sporting.

The fact that neither of the girls was wearing a bra was more visible in Kirsty's case because her white dress allowed her hard dark nipples and areolas to show through. As Fiona entered and saw Fungus's behind, she giggled.

"I see you're beginning to enjoy yourself without me, not fair!"

He winced as she approached him and she caressed his ass with her fingers, feeling the raised welts. She then gave him three firm slaps and a pointed reprimand. She received a leather crop from Kirsty.

Fiona, why don't you catch up, my darling? While I pour us some ready-made chilled Chardonnay, give him twelve with the produce. I'm sure he needs it.' Fungus murmured something, and Kirsty overheard and continued, "In fact, he might need more than twelve, based on his attitude. Give him eighteen; that will get him ready for what's to come!" As Fiona brought Fungus to the other sofa and placed him over the back with his head and arms hanging down, Fungus' lower lip quiver. He was hard-cropped in the middle by her as she raised her arm above her shoulder.

He cried out after being struck on his already sore ass, which just made Fiona use the crop on him twice more quickly. Between the

purple welts, he now had three very crimson stripes that swiftly created elevated ridges to match the ones already there. At each blow, he sobbed, and Fiona said,

Saying "Fungus, Fungus, Fungus..." Are you unable to learn? I will punish you more severely and swiftly the more you scream out. It will be best for you if you keep quiet,' Fungus cried. He clinched his teeth and grunted as Fiona picked up the crop once again, elevated it, and brought it down lower down his ass. The bottom of his ass cheeks received the next four strokes softly. In addition to Kirsty's purple welts, he now had eight stunning raised welts in a deep shade of red.

She stopped as she ran her fingernails over his welts to feel them. He groaned when she said this, "Even the purple ones were hot, really hot." Fiona crossed the preexisting stripes as she elevated the crop once again and brought it down vertically. His grunts became more shrill and urgent when she repeated this four more times. She still had five more, and she would make sure that they were memorable. Speaking to him,

We are down to the final five, so please count them, thank you, and then request the next one. I repeat the stroke if I don't do this, did I make it clear? Fungus whispered a "Yeah" and attempted to nod while he was upside down. When the crop fell diagonally over his ass, Fiona raised her arm and swung her body to bring it down. He stiffened and cried out.

'Onnnnne! Thank you, Miss. May I have another one, please? Fiona responded,

CHAPTER 33

She repeated her strike in the opposite way after saying, "Of course you can, my worm, of course you can." She then moved to the other side. All of the earlier welts on his ass were now crossed by a sizable crimson "X." He sobbed once more, his tears dripping freely and soaking the couch. He broke down,

'Twooooo! Thank you, Miss. May I have another one, please? Fiona grinned and said,

"Fungus, the last three will be incredibly difficult to count since they will be on your thighs, so get ready!"

He grunted as she raised the crop, then slammed it down on him right at the point where his thighs and buttocks meet. He almost straightened out as he cried out in agony, "Three-ee-ee thank you Miss! May I please have another one? She raised the crop once again and lowered it an inch below the previous stroke, landing on his thighs.

His hands shot to his thighs and gripped them tightly as he sobbed hysterically and couldn't stop crying. He didn't count the stroke when Fiona tapped his thighs with the crop; instead, he just held on tight. Three full minutes went by without him giving a count. She hissed,

Poor boy! You have won an additional one, so that one doesn't count. I'll take the stroke again, and you now have three left to go. Fungus cried out,

Yes, Miss, I understand, she said, raising the crop and ruthlessly bringing it down on his leg. "Aaaa-h-h, Four miss!" she yelled.

Thank you, Miss. May I have another one, please? Fiona grinned and struck him once more sharply, "Five miss! Thank you, Miss. May I have another one, please? She said gently,

He nodded as she brought the crop back and twisted well away from him. She then swung around with all of her weight and brought the crop hard down on the sit-spot again. After it, he was instructed to thank her and request to kiss the crop. His hands flew to the crease, and he grunted through gritted teeth.

'Aaaaayyy! Miss! Ssss-s-six! Thank you, Madam. May I kiss the crop, please? She placed the crop in front of his lips, and he kissed it reverently. Fiona then took hold of his hand and helped him rise up. She then led him back to the wall and told him not to move. His legs and ass were covered in an array of elevated, hot-to-the-touch red and purple welts. He was sobbing as he stood there, spilling tears from his face to the ground.

Kirsty had been watching the spectacle from the other sofa and was impressed; she hadn't seen Fungus defeated by someone other than her in a significant way in a long time; she need to allow others to use him more frequently. Fiona approached her, took a sip of the Chardonnay that was sitting on the small table, and then lifted Kirsty into her arms. With their pussies hot and moist from Fungus's beating, the females kissed each other passionately.

They allowed their hands to wander over each other. Fiona had enormous, firm breasts with long, erect nipples that Kirsty found particularly alluring, while Kirsty preferred Fiona's firm, muscular bottom. Fiona carefully pushed up Kirsty's dress as she gave her a

full-body kiss as her hands gripped her ass. Soon, she was grabbing her bare ass cheeks. When Kirsty removed the garment as she motioned for her to, she was left standing in a tiny triangle made of gossamer-like material and held on either side by the thinnest thread sides Fiona had ever seen. The Irish girl stood there in a sheer black Agent Provocateur string as Kirsty helped her take off her clothing.

Fiona forced Kirsty back onto the couch and knelt between her knees. When Kirsty moaned, already turned on from Fungus's beating at both their hands, Fiona began nibbling through the gossamer that passed for underwear. Fiona took the string thong off and was delighted to see Kirsty had entirely shaved, with not a hair to be seen or felt. She recalled that the previous time she had seen her pussy, her auburn locks had just managed to stay out of the sides of her pants due to an unruly tangle. She was the one who had gently recommended to Kirsty that she may benefit from a trip to the all-body stylist at the studios.

She quickly devoured the Scotch, encouraged by the sounds of a girl being pleased, including gasps and moaning. She inserted her finger into Kirsty's hole and carefully played it in and out before liberally drenching it in cunt juice and moving down to her puckered asshole. Fiona massaged her finger at the opening and then pushed it in firmly. It didn't take much force for the finger to break through the sphincter's barrier, and once it was in, she started finger-fucking her with one, then two, and finally three fingers. She bit her labia, yanking them away from the body as she

continued to suck and bite her clitoris. Kirsty eventually experienced a loud, wet orgasm. Hearing all of this, Fungus pondered whether he would ever be permitted to orgasm.

Kirsty gave Fiona a questioning look as she spoke softly in her ear. After giving it some thought, Kirsty nodded in agreement. Fungus was carried to the center of the living room by Fiona, who then stood him there still with his hands on his head. She placed him in a leather harness with straps that could be fastened around his neck, chest, thighs, and hips. It also featured a strap with a metal cock ring and a large leather portion that went under his crotch and up the back to be fastened to the neck strap.

After pushing in a big butt plug that she had greased, she tightened the crotch strap over it and buckled it behind the hip strap after he had slid his cock and balls through the front ring. He was unable to use his hands without her or Kirsty's permission when she fastened wrist cuffs to him and attached those to the thigh straps. He was now blindfolded by Fiona, who massaged his cock and balls slowly while making sure they were both stuffed full of cum! He was perspiring, and his cock's head was a deep purple color as it throbbed and bobbed eagerly.

When Kirsty surprised Fungus with the caning earlier, it wasn't just the pain that had caused his profuse tears; it was also the threat of not having an orgasm for yet another month. She had this well noted on her planner. Fungus was to be afforded relief tonight. Kirsty had the upper hand.

CHAPTER 34

After several hard minutes of wanking him slowly, quickly, and again, Fiona stopped holding his cock in a vice-like grip. She placed him on the floor on a white rug with a deep pile, picked Kirsty up, sat her on his face, and yelled at him to begin eating out the pussy. She also visited the studio stylist to have her pussy hair taken care of; she sported a very thin strip that extended for an inch above her pussy, which she liked to refer to as her own personal landing strip. In the meantime, she licked her fingers and touched her own slit, spreading her own pussy juice. Only on invitation.

She thought to herself that Fungus's erect cock was a good specimen and one she had never encountered before as she lowered herself onto it and nestled herself on it. Nearly everyone in the firm believed that Fungus was only attracted to men, and that his connection with Kirsty was solely business-related. Nevertheless, recent events had made the group of friends, who were now referring to themselves as "The Rescuers," aware of the truth about Fungus. Kirsty had initially encouraged Fiona to partake in their small amusements.

All of this ran through Fiona's head as she pulled Fungus' rigid member around inside of her, stroked her clitoris, and played with her nipples with her other hand while doing so. She began to sweat more and more as the climax drew near. Fungus's cock jerked, and she realized he was forbidden orgasm for the next month. Nevertheless, she also realized that if it weren't for Fungus, Peyton

would have been found dead in some shack and Fred and Stella would be in charge of the business.

She mouthed the word "Please" while looking Kirsty in the eyes, and she received a "Yes" in response. Fiona let herself go at this point; there was no need for restraint. She fucked Fungus quickly and furiously when suddenly the cock twitched hard, her pussy spasmed, and she arrived just as the cock pumped her pussy full of scorching cum; it seemed to go on forever, the culmination of a month of denial. Fiona repeatedly climbed to the summit, descended, and then climbed back up. This caused Kirsty to have her second orgasm of the evening after being sent over the edge by a particularly deft tongue. She and Fiona both fell off Fungus at the same time, curled their bodies tightly around one another, and fell asleep shortly after. Even though Fungus knew he would have to pay for this spontaneous climax, for the moment he was content to enjoy it.

Fran liked the sound of the name "The Rescuers," and she felt good inside knowing she was one of them. Since she couldn't afford the time to travel to her own bungalow in downtown Bangkok, the studios granted her an apartment in the accommodations wing to use instead.

She wasn't expecting anyone and was simply lazing in a basic white cotton thong and a thin loose kaftan top when there was a tap on the door as she sat enjoying a gin and tonic while listening to some jazz. Mary and Chad were standing there with two bottles of white wine and three glasses between them when she

approached the door and opened it. As Chad opened her mouth, it was immediately apparent that there had previously been another bottle.

We thought you might feel a little lonely tonight, so we thought we'd bring you some white wine from Stella's fridge, which we sort of accidentally found when exploring her office. Why don't you welcome us inside before they warm up? Fran called them in while laughing aloud.

When they entered, they both took off their long t-shirts and remained in their underwear—a powder blue thong for Chad and a pair of black lace cheekinis for Mary. The three of them sat down on the sofa to begin drinking wine after Fran removed her kaftan. The first bottle was a Pinot Grigio; after Chad failed to open it after two attempts and collapsed laughing, Mary took it and tried to open it.

She made it open without spilling anything after one unsuccessful attempt and poured three cups. They drank for their own health as well as Peyton's, the board's, and everyone else's. The first bottle was finished quickly, and when they opened the second, a Cabernet Sauvignon, the girls noticed a warm glow emanating from within them. Throughout the course of their conversation, which encompassed everything under the sun, this bottle was likewise emptied.

They weren't quite ready to put the good times to an end, so Fran got up and looked in the refrigerator. She found an unopened bottle of Chardonnay, which they opened and began to drink. By

this point, they were completely unconcerned with anything else and were laughing and falling over one another. Fran accidentally touched the emergency call button when she jumped to help Chad after she slipped and fell on the low table, hurting her head on the sideboard. All the offices and apartments have emergency call buttons for everyone's protection and security.

Mary and Fran helped the friend who had fallen onto the sofa and fell about laughing while doing so. They had were helping Chad up and had missed the blinking red light on the wall panel. The three sprang up when they heard a sudden loud knock on the door; it was well past midnight; who could it be? Fran stepped to the door and peered through the spyhole. Three security personnel were there.

She opened the door but was too inebriated to realize she was only wearing a thong. When Gloria, Amelia, and Dara entered, they realized what had been happening right away. Gloria remarked,

"Ms. Knuppe, you pressed the emergency button, but I can see there is no problem; you women have had a little too much wine," the officer said. Since this is Ms. Knuppe's residence, it reflects poorly on you ladies. This is not good. The three friends pleaded with her to forget what she had seen and to leave, urging her to just walk out and forget what she had seen. She remained still, her arms crossed, and gave them a stern expression.

The three companions were standing in a group quietly, suddenly mindful of their undress, as Amelia and Dara were staring at the girls and conversing with each other in Filipino.

CHAPTER 35

They also spoke to Gloria, who answered and shook her head. Gloria addressed the trio.

The three friends stood there with their mouths open as Gloria, Dara, and Amelia went behind them and handcuffed them; Fran pleaded with them, repeating that it had been an accident, that they had gotten drunk because they had been so nervous during Peyton's absence, and that it had been an accident. "I am afraid my colleagues are right, the setting off of the alarm was an act of wanton vandalism," Gloria said. "I have to take you ladies in until the Chairman can discuss your case with

The guards began to leave while carrying one of the three females, who began to scream and plead not to leave like this because they were almost naked. Amelia and Dara nodded and laughed gleefully as Gloria paused and spoke in Filipino. The three of them exchanged shocked glances as they turned the females around and brought them back to the sofa.

Their heads dropped forward as the guards led them to the back of the sofa and tipped them against the backrest. Gloria had Mary, Dara had Chad, and Amelia had Fran in front of her. The three guards unbuckled their service belts, removed their leather belts from the hooks on their pants, snapped the leather, and raised their arms in the air. The three girls shouted and grumbled as they continued to be strapped, right on their buttocks, at Gloria's signal. Gloria spoke after it had ceased.

"My girls find you all extremely attractive but a little spoilt, and we think you need a good strapping. We also think you deserve a good lesbian fuck, which we are prepared to offer to you. We have decided that it might be easier for everyone if we just settled this between us now." So just take in this and keep in mind that if you decide not to participate, let us know so we can send you to the jail. Yeah, and if you keep screaming, I'll assume you prefer to be locked up.

As Gloria signaled them to take off their little underwear, the girls on the sofa murmured their assent and resumed strapping. The belts were made of thick, high-quality leather that was two inches wide and pliable from use. The guards pressed them down on the ladies' bottoms with all of their strength.

Each had their own distinctive style: Gloria kept her belt long and single thickness and simply continued belting steadily without pausing or stopping; Dara doubled her belt and hit hard with long pauses between strokes; Amelia also doubled hers and then laid two strokes in rapid succession followed by a long pause before the next two.

Ten minutes later, they came to a stop, and the guards switched places, picking up a new girl to strap. The three friends begged for forgiveness while the guards alternated the girls every ten minutes. Each lady had been thoroughly strapped twice by each guard after an hour, at which point their rears were bright red from the middle of the buttocks to the top of the thigh and they continued to wriggle on the back of the sofa.

Gloria straightened Fran and spoke softly to her once the punishment ended as the girls simply sat there sobbing and crying their eyes out.

We need three strap-ons, and I'm sure you have some here. If not, I'll have to go to my own quarters where I have some extra-large ones I use with my experienced friends.' Fran nodded and took her to the bedroom, where she instructed Gloria to check a suitcase she had stashed in the closet. In fact, among other toys, she discovered three gorgeous strap-ons inside the bag. They returned to the living room, where Fran was once more slung over the sofa's back.

Gloria wore a reasonable full-cup white cotton bra and high knickers, while Amelia wore a seductive lacy purple satin three-quarter bra and tanga. The guards undressed to their underwear. Dara was the smallest and wore a very sensual half cup bra with red lace and a red and black string that was completely over the top. They each took a strap-on and adjusted it to fit before lubricating the cocks and placing them against the three pairs of labia that were on display.

Fran was in front of Amelia as she gently prodded the wet pussy with the blue silicone dildo and easefully moved it in a little at a time. Fran let out a long, soft groan. Amelia gradually increased the sensation by pushing Fran's hurting ass until the harness was right up against it.

Dara and Chad were put together, and the assistant pushed the convincing-looking cock into Dara's pussy while it was actually

oozing. She pushed it all the way to the rubber balls in one rapid motion, stopped it there so Chad could get a feel for it, and then slowly pulled it out while positioned at the labia, once more going directly to the balls. Chad resumed this action, groaning and gasping with each stroke.

Gloria had Mary, and she was sporting a monstrous strap-on, thick and veined, that looked nothing like a genuine cock and was made of black silicone and fastened to a leather harness with studs. When she put it against the Thai's hot pussy hole after thoroughly lubricating it, it only inserted half an inch; after another push, it inserted the remaining half inch. Gloria grabbed Mary by the waist and gave her a firm push, which caused the cock to slide in two inches and cause Mary to groan and sob. Perhaps it was too much, because when Gloria took the cock out an inch, there was a smear of fresh blood on it. Gloria pushed in again, this time three inches, because she was confident Mary could handle it.

It took some time, but once the entire cock was within, Mary felt as though she may burst. She cried out in response to each thrust, and soon tears were running down her face. The guards cheered each other on as they rode the girls to a climax while the three girls made noises that ranged from moans to grunts to sobs and tears poured freely.

The strap-ons were utilized on the girls' asses at various points throughout the night as the guards switched out the girls, some of whom were more compliant than others.

CHAPTER 36

Fran, an anal erotic who adored being taken there, had a very flexible ass compared to Mary's, which was very tight. Chad, who was new to anal, handled the pain reasonably well, with no complaints. The guards were now toying with their own nipples after removing their bras and gleefully fisted the girls.

The females were strapped and raped by all three guards as it was getting close to morning, and they were now asleep while their asses were deep red and covered with pussy juice on the rug and sofa. The fake cocks were lying around the room like toys after the guards had used the strap-ons on each other for their own amusement.

Beta reclined on her bed and played with her nipples while watching the enormous 52-inch television mounted on the wall of her bedroom. She wore a leather harness that framed her large tits and shaved pussy. She was smiling to herself as three gorgeous young girls—her young girls—began severely beating three sexy women who were handcuffed and lying face down over the back of the sofa.

There was no area of the studios she couldn't look into because she had been given free reign to install security cameras and alarms wherever and however she pleased. She had employed a very small and quiet business, and certain feeds were obviously encrypted so that only Beta could view them. Just what she was doing at the moment.

In order to hear the sound of leather against flesh and the cries of pain, which both turned her on so much, she turned up the volume. When she sucked her pussy out, she reached down and grabbed Bea's curly hair. She then pushed Bea over her pussy and forced her to rub her face into it.

Due to a specific "misunderstanding" with a male instructor during her final year, Bea, her youngest and favorite recruit fresh out of the navy academy, was unable to pursue a military career. He tried to compel her, but she refused, biting the tip off and feeding it to the piranhas he kept in an aquarium. Because of Beta, who was a close friend of Vita, the camp commandant's wife, who had Beta's name tattooed on her pussy, Bea was rescued from the stockade. The sole requirement was for Beta to take Bea and use her, which she duly did. The male teacher was last spotted leaving for work at the Philippine Antarctic Station in a military vehicle.

Bea is a 22-year-old 100% lesbian with a stunning figure, and boy did she devour pussy! Beta simply reclined and watched the action on the screen while playing with her engorged nipples as she was being transported to heaven and beyond with every lick and suck.

Bea used to meticulously and skillfully shave her pussy every day. Nothing made her happier than to let Beta lie on the bed naked while she gently lathered her with warm water and shaving foam, shaved her, and made sure no stray hairs were left behind. After removing any remaining suds, she would cleanse the pussy with a warm, wet face cloth before applying soothing aloe gel to every nook and crevice.

Bea was Beta's protégé, her little pet, and her favorite. Beta drew Bea close to her and gave her a passionate kiss. There were approximately twenty security guards working for the company, divided into five teams of four, but Beta had her favorite team, comprised of Gloria, Dara, Amelia, and Bea. She had slept with all four at one point, occasionally alone and occasionally in various combinations. Naturally, she had recorded every session and would replay them whenever she was bored. Although Bea gave her a full face kiss, she was preoccupied with her thoughts. In order to see the television again, she pushed herself down to her nipples.

The situation had altered; from what she could see, her three guards had put on strap-ons and were giving the three pals a good fucking! Bea was pulled up next to her so she could watch with her. The two women sat up in bed and watched as Beta roughly touched Bea's nipples. She became more horny and anxious to pierce the willing recruit with each push of the strap-ons.

Bea's eyes shot wide as Beta sprang from the bed and ran to the restroom. When she returned, she was wearing a black harness and a huge, genuine black cock that had veins. Beta shouted,

'Bea! Now get down on all fours! We are coming! She approached the bed where Bea was curled up facing the screen on all fours. While waiting for her mistress, she hung her head low. Suddenly, she felt a push in her wet pussy that grew harder and harder by the second as it slipped in with ease. Her hymen was long gone, but Bea's pussy was still young and tight. She had been repeatedly

CHAPTER 37

They were both watching the scene play out on the TV, and it almost appeared as though they were a part of it. Beta hammered the young ass as her little friend squealed with joy. The young girl was now crying out in time with the thrusts and once more she could feel an impending orgasm as Beta sank her nails into her thighs and drew her towards her body. The strap-on Beta was wearing featured a panel of raised nodules and rubber studs right where it met her clitoris; the harder she thrust, the harder her own pussy got pummeled. Beta was about to have her own climax.

Bea shouted and moaned as the fucking sent her on a one-way trip to her climax. The two women were grunting like pigs as they steadily drew closer to their orgasm. She suddenly became quiet... five... ten... fourteen minutes. She suddenly let out a howl and started to move forward relentlessly, bucking like a bronco. Beta's joy at witnessing her pet experience climax drove her over the edge; she came with a long, low groan before falling back.

Beta turned off the television and then settled down with Bea; their personal encounter had also been captured on camera and she would doubtless view it at a later time, perhaps while having sex with someone else. As they both gradually fell asleep, she played with Bea's hair, allowing Beta to dream of dominating attractive young ladies and Bea to fantasize of being restrained and thrashed by a powerful woman. Whatever you desire it to be, that is heaven.

After a week...

Peyton was perfectly dressed in a navy suit, a skirt that was just above the knee, a starched white blouse, very sheer stockings that were almost black, and high heeled Louboutins as she stood at the head of the boardroom table. She was speaking in a loud, clear voice that was actually her best teaching voice.

"Ladies and gentlemen, I have deemed it essential to convene an emergency board meeting for this morning due to recent occurrences. Two of our board members have died while they were being tried for kidnapping and torturing me. Because of this, I have taken decisions that I will now share with you all after consulting with my remaining director, the company accountant, and our assistants.' Many in attendance pressed forward to hear better; some knew some of what was coming while others knew nothing; nobody knew all.

Peyton continued, "I've decided to create the position of Deputy Director and promoted Ms. Mary Watt to this position. She will represent me while I'm away, and Chad will continue to be her assistant. Ms. Fran Knuppe is being promoted to Director in Charge of Staff, and Ms. Teresa Banham will be her assistant. The new Director in Charge of Production will be Ms. Inge Müller, who used to be the studio manager, and her assistant will be Mr. Nuno Soare Ms. Juliette Gréco, who has previously worked in the general typing pool, will assume the role of Secretary to the Board. I now have Ms. Fiona Samuel as my personal assistant.

When the new board members knocked and the door opened to let them in, everyone in the room mixed and chatted before Peyton

grabbed her documents and invited everyone to some beverages and snacks that had been prepared beforehand. Peyton was approached by Mary, who handed her a glass of champagne and remarked,

"Peyton, my friend, my lover, my sub, you came to my nation and walked into a completely new life, a life I think you appreciate and will enjoy for many years to come," I said. What are your plans now that you are the owner and managing director of a multi-million dollar company? Will you remain? Will you return to the United States? As she responded, Peyton gave her companion a gentle touch on the face.

"Mary, Mistress, friend, lover, my life has completely changed. I now find myself the multi-millionaire owner and Managing Director of a pornographic film studios. I have also learned that I have a strong interest in sex issues and simply want to make up for lost time. I have to return to New York because I have things to take care of there, and I also need time away from here to plan my next move. I've asked Fiona to arrange for a flight to Newark for tomorrow evening. Will you have time to represent me in person while I'm there? Peyton said to Mary, "While I spoke to you, my hand had fallen down and was tenderly caressing the Thai girl's arms and breasts."

Mary told Peyton, "Peyton, I had already thought about leaving my post in the police, but now that I've been promoted, the decision is firm.

CHAPTER 38

I'll write my resignation letter in the next few days and deliver it personally to my chief." Peyton was delighted to hear this news and tightly hugged and kissed Mary.

"Mary, before I return to Manhattan, I want to spend the night with you in your small cottage and let you use and abuse me. I want the proof of your abuse to be visible when I look in my mirror in Manhattan. I want my ass, my tits, and my body to suffer and to display the stripes and welts you have given me. I won't be able to decide what I have to do till then.' Mary clenched her lover and nodded. She gave her a gentle kiss and responded,

We will depart now while the others continue to converse. The following day, I will drive you to the airport and personally bid you farewell because I want to be the one to do it. Out the door, now! Just as Mary predicted, nobody barely noticed they were gone, and two hours later they were back at Mary's bungalow. They let themselves in and undressed, still perspiring even with the air conditioning on the way home from the car. Although Mary was sporting a daring half-bra and thong in yellow with black polka dots, Peyton was sporting a lacy lilac bra and knickers combination. Both women left wearing their shoes: Mary was wearing a pair of light blue espadrille wedges and Peyton was wearing her Louboutins. They reclined on the sofa for a bit to unwind as Mary poured drinks for the two.

After some time, Mary came in close to Peyton and gave her a soft, all-over kiss, including butterfly kisses on her lips and

eyelids. Peyton made to kiss him back when she was greeted with an intense slap on the face; her cheeks turned crimson, and tears welled up in her eyes. She tenderly stroked her face and held her head while he kissed her. Mary delivered her another hard slap on the other cheek almost immediately after that. Then, in a fit of wrath, she stood up, grabbed Peyton by the ear, and pulled her wailing and crying down into the dungeon.

A small velvet-covered cushion was then pushed under Peyton just in contact with her pussy mound before using a restraint Peyton had never seen before. This restraint was attached to both sides of the bed, and when Mary tightened it there was no way Peyton could raise her body off the bed or even move from side to side. Peyton felt pressure from the cushion on her bladder but ignored it.

Mary left her there for a short while while she went upstairs. After a short while, she started to feel pretty thirsty and dizzy, so she assumed the drink must already be starting to take effect. Peyton drank quickly from Mary's sports bottle with a flexible straw when she returned, and as her thirst grew worse, she continued to drink until the bottle was empty. When Mary gave her a second bottle, Peyton accepted it while remaining just as thirsty as before. Halfway through her third bottle, after finishing the second one, she suddenly had the desire to urinate.

Mary, could you kindly let me go, I have to use the restroom.

Peyton was anticipating Mary to unbuckle her when her ass erupted in flames.

CHAPTER 39

Mary repeatedly brought her strap down on the exposed ass as she gave her a stern look. Peyton screamed and begged for mercy as the blows continued to fall on her. The urge to urinate became excruciating, so she contracted her bladder muscles to prevent any leaks. Mary's voice was soft.

You won't be able to sit on the way back home because you will be so sore. "Don't you dare wet my bed because if you do I will beat you to within an inch of your life!"

She then resumed hitting Peyton in the behind and knee-deep in the backs of her thighs. She started pleading for permission to urinate since the cushion was exerting such intense pressure on her bladder that it was asking to be emptied.

Peyton was startled and began frantically shaking her head when Mary stopped striking her and revealed a new bottle of beverage. After closing Peyton's nostrils with a nose clip, Mary placed a mouthpiece with a funnel over her mouth and fastened it with Velcro behind her head. After a few seconds, Peyton was forced to swallow since she would otherwise suffocate from the contents of the bottle. After pouring the contents of a second bottle into Peyton's stomach, Mary removed the mouthpiece and grinned at her.

As the pains came on in waves and it became more and more difficult for her to hold it in, she sobbed and pleaded to be let go. Peyton grew pale as Mary lifted the thick, heavy-duty Lochgelly three-tailed tawse to her shoulder and then brought it down with

all of her weight behind it. Mary had reached down to show Peyton what was in her hands. Every ten seconds, a blow would come steadily from the left, right, left, and right with no alternate cheeks, sounding like an explosion and being followed by a scream.

Peyton just needed six strokes until the dam gave way, her bladder could no longer withstand the strain, and she totally soaked herself while sobbing uncontrollably.

Peyton was dragged to a corner of the dungeon where Mary lowered the tawse and freed her. There, she reattached the wrist cuffs to a hanging hook and raised it until the unfortunate girl was standing on tiptoes. Then, using a long, whippy cane, she began to beat the woman all over, starting from the back and working her way down through the buttocks, thighs, and knees to the back of her abdomen. Next came the tits, of course, but Mary here paid particular attention to the nipples, making sure she caught them with the most severe strokes. The pussy mound was the last to be reached; here, with each stroke, pussy juice squirted out and formed stunning stripes.

She had a mass of gorgeous stripes covering her entire body, front and back, from her knees to her shoulders; she would have to pick her outfits for the next few weeks very carefully! The stripes changed color as the caning went on, turning stronger red, then purple, and ultimately becoming raised welts.

After twenty minutes of brutal beating, Peyton passed out. Mary freed her from her restraints and carefully carried her upstairs. She

placed Peyton on the bed and then sat next to her as she slept till she felt ready to return to society. After a little while, the American woke up, so Mary scooped her up and brought her to the bathroom where she carefully bathed, oiled, and perfumed the woman before carrying her back to the bed and finally resting down next to her while they both drifted off to sleep.

Peyton had nightmares about nuns, beatings, Fred, and Jerry. She also had nightmares about whips, canes, and pricks, both real and silicone. At some point during the night, she also had an orgasm, likely aided by a fingering that she wasn't sure was real or part of her dream. Eventually, Peyton fell asleep and didn't wake up until Mary gently shook her and gave her a kiss and some fresh orange juice.

Together, Peyton and Mary had a shower and had breakfast of fresh fruit, croissants, and coffee before Peyton had to go. The journey was over.

Or perhaps the adventure had just started.

THE END

CPSIA information can be obtained
at www.ICGtesting.com
Printed in the USA
LVHW041557200423
744868LV00001B/7

9 781804 347812